THERE'S A NEW WITCH IN TOWN

A HOLIDAY HILLS WITCH COZY MYSTERY

CAROLYN RIDDER ASPENSON

Severn River
PUBLISHING

THERE'S A NEW WITCH IN TOWN

Severn River Publishing
www.SevernRiverPublishing.com

ISBN: 978-1-64875-913-0 (Paperback)

The Lily Sprayberry Realtor Cozy Mystery Series

Deal Gone Dead

Decluttered and Dead

Signed, Sealed and Dead

Bidding War Break-In

Open House Heist

Realtor Rub Out

Foreclosure Fatality

Lily Sprayberry Novellas

The Scarecrow Snuff Out

The Claus Killing

Santa's Little Thief

The Chantilly Adair Paranormal Cozy Mystery Series

Get Up and Ghost

Ghosts Are People Too

Praying For Peace

Ghost From the Grave

Haunting Hooligans: A Chantilly Adair Novella

The Pooch Party Cozy Mystery Series

Pooches, Pumpkins, and Poison

Hounds, Harvest, and Homicide

Dogs, Dinners, and Death

The Holiday Hills Witch Cozy Mystery Series

There's a New Witch in Town

Witch This Way

Who's That Witch?

The Magical Real Estate Mystery Series

Spooks for Sale

Selling Spells Trouble

Cloaked Commission

The Angela Panther Mystery Series

Unfinished Business

Unbreakable Bonds

Uncharted Territory

Unexpected Outcomes

Unbinding Love

The Christmas Elf

The Ghosts

Undetermined Events

The Event

The Favor

Undesirable Situations

Magical Real Estate Mystery Series

Other Books

Mourning Crisis (The Funeral Fakers Series)

Join Carolyn's Newsletter List at

CarolynRidderAspenson.com

You'll receive a free novella as a thank you!

For Lynn Shaw
Thank you for taking this journey with me.
You rock, woman!

CHAPTER 1

*E*veryone has a crazy aunt, right? The kind of woman that takes their niece on exciting trips to fascinating places like Disney or on shopping sprees in New York City. An aunt who plays dress up with her, lets her explore her drawer full of makeup, even teaches her how to use it at too young of an age. Those aunts give the most amazing Christmas presents. They teach their niece the things her mother would flip out over if she knew.

Everyone loves that aunt.

I don't have an aunt, but my mother, Addie Odell, she fit the bill perfectly. Having a crazy aunt is one thing, but having a crazy mother? That's a lot of work.

Okay, I'll admit, the dress up, the makeup experimentation, the spontaneous, fascinating trips—crazy and wonderful—were some of the best times of my life, for sure. The problem was, my mother lacked basic mothering skills, and let's face it, a kid needs those. We were more like friends, partners in what she called the crime of life, but in the long run, I thought I turned out okay.

All of that aside, the worst thing my mother-who-should-have-been-my-aunt gave me was a Christmas gift, and trust me, it was a doozy.

"You're a witch," Addie Odell mumbled, her voice low, rough, and barely audible. "Just like me, Abigail. You're just like me."

My head buzzed back and forth. Did she just call me the b-word? "Mom, I'm sorry." I leaned forward, my ear close to her face. "I'm sorry Mom, say that again."

She lightly squeezed my hand with her frail, weak fingers. "A witch. Don't let them take your magic, sweet Abby." Her words came out strong and clear, like before she'd gotten sick. I hadn't heard such clarity in her speaking for months.

I'm a *what*? The delirious minds of the dying are filled with illusions, hallucinations, memories that aren't real, and jumbled, rambled thoughts. I assumed my mother's comments were one of those. I was not a witch. And neither was my mother. Witches lived only in fiction; the kind of fiction I wrote, actually.

She died in her sleep that night, a night when she assured me she was on an upswing, and after she forced me to go home and get a good night's sleep in my own bed. She must have been having a strange dream to say such a silly thing, she'd said, waving it off like a random thought. And against my better judgement, I did as she asked. I went home that night.

* * *

Most of Holiday Hills came out for Adaline Odell's life celebration. She'd planned it herself, years ago, claiming such an event should never be left to the grief stricken, for they could not see things the way the dying could, and weren't capable of the proper way to honor the dead. I had no idea what that meant until I walked into the funeral home.

Oliver Remington, the funeral home director, escorted me to my mother's viewing room. When he opened the door, I stopped dead in my tracks, no pun intended. "I…I…" I shook my head. "I'm sorry to appear disrespectful, but did a floral shop throw up in here?"

He chuckled and his rather large belly bounced up and down on his short body. "Adaline said you'd say something like that, and she asked that I remind you of her love for roses."

I took in a deep breath through my mouth instead of my nose, and tasted the silky, sweet rose smell on my tongue. "Yes, I'm aware of her obsession, but wow. What if we have guests who are allergic? Or people that aren't allergic but are overwhelmed and sneeze through her service? I'm concerned this is a bit much, Mr. Remington." I rubbed beneath my nose. The power of influence our minds have over us is amazing. I didn't have an allergy to flowers, but my nose immediately itched.

The lights flickered. We both glanced up at them, but they stayed on.

He smiled, a full face, teeth showing smile. "Miss. Odell, your mother also assured me the flowers wouldn't be an issue for anyone." He coughed. "As for the lights, I'll check on them. Let's hope it's not a ghost."

I pressed my lips together, thinking he was probably kidding, but what funeral director cracked jokes like that? "That's fine, and well then, a room flooded with roses it is." My nose itched again, so I scratched it.

I'll give you a moment—"

The lights flickered again. My eyes widened, and Mr. Remington nodded.

"I'll check on that now."

I approached my mother's coffin slowly and wiped a tear from my eye as I touched her silky black hair one last time. I missed her and her crazy antics so much. I missed her eccentric sense of style, the way she couldn't care less what others thought of her seventies styled hippy clothes. I especially missed her keen intuition. She'd helped me with so much in my life, and I'd grown to rely on her ability to know the answers at the exact moment I needed them. If not for that, I would have never discovered my ex-husband's betrayal, and heaven knows where I'd be now.

Zach wasn't a bad guy, he just wasn't the guy for me. Wait, maybe that wasn't the right way to say it. It was more that I wasn't the right girl for Zach. Then again, from what I'd learned, pretty much every girl but me was the right girl for Zach, at least while we were married anyway.

"Oh, Mom, what will I do without you?" I swallowed back the lump in my throat and used a tissue to wipe the little drip coming from my nose.

Out of nowhere the Eagles, "There's a New Kid in Town" exploded from the speakers in the room. The song was my mother's favorite. Seconds later, the music stopped, but I sung the opening lyrics to myself anyway as a life full of music and memories flooded my mind.

Mr. Remington quietly entered again. "Ms. Odell, my apologies. It seems we're having a bit of a glitch with our electrical system. I've got someone on it now, and I promise you we'll have it fixed in a few minutes."

"Oh, thank you. I'm...I'm sure it won't be an issue."

* * *

My mother's viewing reminded me of my wedding reception. Everyone greeted me in a line, sharing a story and a hug about my mom. Tears caught in the crinkles of our smiles as we laughed at shared memories.

Addie Odell always said she wanted to go out with a bang. "When I kick the bucket, I don't want one of those sad funerals where everyone dresses in black and bawls their eyes out. I want a party. I want you all to celebrate my life because it's been a party itself."

She'd set it up to be just that, and that's what we'd had, disco music and all, and when K.C. from K.C. and the Sunshine Band arrived to perform, the crowd cheered.

My mother somehow convinced a 70s disco singer to bid her

farewell at her viewing. Who didn't love that? Everyone in the room thought it was a hoot, and that's exactly what my mother intended, no doubt. I couldn't help myself. I bawled my eyes out. My nose ran like crazy, and I knew it would be ridiculously red from all the sandpaper like tissue the funeral home provided.

The power issue was never fixed. Every few minutes the lights flicked and a few even blew. The loudspeaker screamed two more Eagles songs, but they managed to shut it off quickly. It didn't matter though. Everyone just considered it part of my mother's plan.

Since Mom had no intention of being interred in the family tomb with a crowd surrounding her, including me, we said our final goodbyes and left for refreshments and snacks in the parlor of the funeral home. I wanted to go to the tomb, but I followed my mother's wishes.

"This isn't a goodbye," she'd said. "And if you watch them put my human remains in that tomb, you'll just waste your makeup."

As if my makeup wasn't already a hot mess.

A wrinkled old woman I'd never met approached me. Her long black dress flowed behind her like a short lacy train. Fly away dangles from her long silvery hair wisped around her face. She blew them away.

"Abigail, dear." She held my hand and a buzz of electricity shot through my body when we touched.

I stepped back and tried to pull away, but she wouldn't let go.

"Be careful, child. Your power is stronger than your mother knew."

"I'm sorry, my what?"

She dropped my hand. "In time, my dear. In time." She turned to walk away as my best friend Stella walked over.

"How you holding up?"

I stared down at my hand, flipping it over and over. The old woman's touch still buzzing through my skin.

"What's wrong? Did you hurt your hand?"

Stella crossed the line to over-compensating mode the minute I told her my mom died. I appreciated how much she cared, but twenty-seven isn't exactly the age for friend-mothering, and I wanted to take care of myself. "I'm fine. I just…that woman, she just said the weirdest thing to me, and when she touched my hand, this, I don't know…this bolt of electricity or something shot through me."

Stella raised her eyebrow. "What woman?"

"The woman I was just talking to."

"Uh…" Her blank stare told me she didn't have a clue what I was talking about.

"You literally walked up as she was walking away."

She glanced behind her and then back at me. "Uh, you've had a long day. Maybe you should sit down."

I scoped out the room. Most everyone had left, and I had a good view of the space, but a double check did no good. The old woman was gone. "She must have already left." I took a napkin from one of the tables and blew my nose. The roses did a number on me.

A vase full of white roses next to a pitcher of iced tea toppled over.

I rushed over and set it upright before the water soaked the carpet.

Stella followed behind. "Right." She patted my shoulder. "Anyway, Mr. Remington said they'll clean everything up in here. Do you want to head over to The Enchanted?"

"What about the flowers?" I rubbed my nose. "I'm definitely not taking any home. They're already messing with my nose and I'm not even in the room with most of them."

The lights flickered again.

I looked up at the ceiling. "I really hope they get that taken care of."

"Right? And by flowers do you mean the pop up rose garden

in the other room?" She chuckled. "Already taken care of." She pushed a long spiral blonde curl behind her ear.

What I wouldn't give for those curls. I gazed past her, my eyes focused on nothing. "Oh, okay."

She waved her hand in front of my face. "You in there?"

"Yeah, I'm sorry. It's been a long few days."

"I know." She wrapped her arm around my shoulders. "It gets easier, I promise."

Stella knew. She'd lost her mother a few years ago. I thought I understood then, but in retrospect, I hadn't. No one understood that kind of loss until they experienced it themselves.

* * *

Bessie, my mother's lifetime best friend and owner of The Enchanted, a book shop that subbed as Holiday Hills' favorite local coffee shop, waved as we walked up. She'd just flipped The Enchanted's sign from closed to open. "Hey sweetie, I was hoping you'd come by." She wrapped me into a tight hug. "How are you doing?"

Everyone in town loved Bessie, but they especially loved The Enchanted. I loved them both equally. Bessie had been around since I could remember and filled in the holes of parenting my mother left open. She tutored me in math, made sure my school projects were done on time. All the things my mother thought weren't important, Bessie handled.

The old bookstore with its mismatched bookshelves stuffed with both new and used books, some of them first editions, and the used but comfy leather chairs gave the store that lived in family room appeal people loved. It was the local hang out, where people met to chat. I spent my days working there, considering it my personal office.

My mother loved The Enchanted, too, so much so she helped Bessie keep the store running. It always struck me as odd that no one ever bought books there. Sure, they bought coffee and the occasional baked item or basic sandwich Bessie whipped up, but rarely did I see a book or magazine bagged and sent away with someone to love it. I wasn't sure how Bessie kept the place open on coffee sales at a buck a cup, but maybe she wasn't in it for the money.

I sighed. "I'm okay." That wasn't a lie. I was okay, at least for the most part. Confused maybe, and definitely a little lost, but in the whole scope of things, okay.

"Well good." She turned the sign back to closed. "Come on. I'll get you a cup of hot tea."

"You don't have to stay closed. I'm fine, really."

"I want to give you some time if you need it."

"No, really, I'm okay. I just want things to get back to normal, you know? And that includes keeping The Enchanted open."

She gave me a quick smile and a wink and flipped the sign over one last time.

Mr. Charming greeted me in his usual way. "Hello, pretty girl. Pretty girl."

"Hello, Mr. Charming." I rubbed my nose against his hard beak. "You look handsome today."

"Mr. Charming's handsome. Handsome."

Mr. Charming was my mom's pet parrot. Like Bessie, he'd been around as long as I could remember, chatting away, and sticking right by my mom's side practically everywhere she went.

Stella groaned. "Five years. I've known this parrot for five years, and he's never once greeted me."

"He greets you all the time." I held out my arm for the green parrot to perch. He did a half fly half jump over from his spot on the counter. "Mr. Charming, say hello to Stella."

"Hello. Hello."

"See?"

"He says that to everyone. I meant he doesn't greet me with something personal like hello gorgeous or something."

I laughed. "He'll be spending a lot more time with me, so maybe I'll teach him."

"I'd appreciate that."

Bessie poured us each a cup of tea and we sat at my table. It wasn't officially my table, but it was the one I worked at daily, and I'd kind of grown attached to it. Mr. Charming perched himself back on the counter once more. "You two probably aren't hungry. That was a lot of food at your momma's celebration," she said.

Stella rubbed her non-existent belly. "I'm not sure I'll ever eat again."

"Well you should. You could use some meat on those bones."

Wasn't that the truth? Stella prided herself on her fit physique. She always said her petite size showed weight faster than my nearly six-foot amazon figure. She worked out daily to stay in shape and regularly attempted to drag me to the gym. I'd gone kicking and screaming a few times, but the aftermath left me whiny and sore, and it just wasn't worth it. "I'm good, but thanks."

A flash of light outside zipped by the front window. I caught a glimpse of it as it passed. "Did you see that?" I pointed to the window as I nudged Stella.

"What?" She stared toward the front windows.

"A weird light just went flying by the window."

"Huh. I missed it. Maybe it was lightning or something."

In December? Not likely in northern Georgia.

She added a packet of Stevia to her coffee. "So, you think Cooper's going to adjust to having Mr. Charming around?"

"They've spent a lot of time together. I'm sure it'll be fine."

"Yes, but this is a full-time gig now, and Cooper is pretty attached to you."

She was right. My little silky brick Burmese cat did have a teeny unhealthy attachment, but I'd created that, so I couldn't blame him. "I'm going to be the divorced woman with a house full of animals and no social life, let alone boyfriend."

"You are not. You've just got your own little zoo now. Maybe you'll meet a Steve Irwin type. You know, someone that loves animals."

"Right." I sipped my coffee and scanned the shelves of books in the café store. They reminded me of my looming deadline and my inability to focus on my work in progress. "I really need to get that book done." I sniffled. Either all the crying I'd done in the last week, or the makeshift rose garden at my mother's celebration of life stuffed my nose so much even a Costco sized box of tissue wouldn't help.

"Are you getting sick?" She whistled to Bessie. "Can we get a napkin here?"

"Stella."

She waved it off. "She knows I'm kidding. I'm not that bossy."

"Right."

Bessie brought over a napkin. "Here you go sweetie. You do sound awful. Maybe you need some Nyquil or something?"

I smirked at Stella. "Told you."

She shrugged.

I rubbed my nose. "Thank you, Bessie. I don't have time for Nyquil. I've got a deadline."

Stella groaned. "Girl, that is the last thing you need to worry about right now."

Gas flames lit up the small fireplace at the front of the store.

"Woah," Stella said. "How'd that happen?"

Bessie glanced at the fireplace, then at me and tilted her head to the side, then eyed the fireplace once again. "That thing's been acting up lately." She winked at us. "Excuse me."

Merlock Dupe, the crankiest man in Holiday Hills, arrived a few minutes before and was just settling into his seat. Obviously, he didn't care about the closed sign on the door. "What in the devil?"

While the man wouldn't win any nicest man of the year

award, I saw something gentle, something sad even, in his dark brown eyes. They spoke of loss, of loneliness. Maybe his crankiness had to do with that?

Bessie waved him off and lowered the gas flame. "Calm down, Merlock."

Stella set a pair of stern eyes on me. "About that deadline. It can wait."

"Wrong. It's in two weeks and I'm not even at a thousand words."

As a ghostwriter for a bestselling cozy mystery author—and I use author even though technically she doesn't write a word of the story—I had fairly strict deadlines to follow.

"Um, I think the publisher will understand." She leaned back in her seat. "Just ask for an extension."

"I can't. They've already started promoting the darn thing, and it's got a pre-order on Amazon. If I don't get it done, B.K. will pitch a fit."

"B.K. can stuff it. You know how I feel about her."

I touched my finger to my chin. "Let me think. Something like a lazy, half-baked, pretend bestselling author without a leg to stand on? Am I right?"

Her upper lip twitched. "Pretty close, minus a few expletives." Stella blamed her colorful vocabulary on her Chicago roots, but she'd made a resolution for the new year to give up swearing, and because she thought it would be nearly impossible, started practicing a month early. She was already failing miserably, but I kept my lips zipped about that.

Another light whizzed by the front window.

"Did you see that?"

She followed my finger and glanced at the front of the store. "See what?"

"That light."

Her eyes shifted from me to the window and then to me again. "Seriously Abby, you need some rest."

I chalked it up to a long few days and an overactive imagination and scooted my chair closer to her side of the small round table. "Can I tell you something?"

She crooked her head. "Of course."

"That lady, she said something strange to me."

"What lady?"

"The one I told you about, in the black dress?"

"Okay." She stretched out the *a* sound in the word.

"She said I need to be careful."

"Alright. Of?"

"Okay, this is going to sound crazy, but my mom said something to me, and I didn't think anything of it, but then this woman, and the weird energy, and now I'm wondering what—"

She pressed her hands onto the tabletop. "Breathe Ab, breathe."

I took a deep breath and exhaled slowly.

"Good, now start from the beginning. Your mother said what and when?"

I doubled up on the deep breaths before speaking. "She said I'm a witch."

Stella laughed. "You sure she didn't mean a b—"

I cut her off and widened my eyes, staring right into hers. "I'm serious."

She pressed her lips together.

"I know this sounds crazy, and I didn't think anything of it, seriously, but then that woman, she just appeared out of…out of nowhere and tells me to be careful because my power is stronger than my mother thought, and then she just disappeared."

"You're right. That does sound crazy."

"But it's true." I crossed my heart. "Honestly."

Stella crossed her heart, too. "I didn't see a woman at the funeral home."

Bessie organized a pile of books on a nearby table, so I kept my voice low. "You don't have to believe me, but it's true."

"Honey, your mom was really sick, you know that, and I've heard that people who are close to death have hallucinations and stuff." She tilted her head. "So maybe…"

"I know, but you weren't there. She spoke like…like she was her old self."

Her chest expanded and then she released a long, slow breath. "Ab—"

I waved my hands at her. "Forget it. It's nothing. I'm just not myself at the moment."

"No, you're not, and you won't be for a while, but that's okay." She continued on like I hadn't just said something obscure. "Right before my mom passed she had this burst of energy, and she was you know, normal. It was like she didn't have cancer, like she was her old self. She died a few hours later, and the hospice nurse told me that happens a lot with people who are sick. They get one last surge of life and then they're gone."

I knew I sounded crazy, and Stella was right. Maybe I was tired. I had every reason to be. "I'm exhausted."

"I know. You really need to email your editor. She'll understand."

* * *

Cooper greeted me at the door with a full-bodied rub between my legs. That was probably more for him than me, but I still enjoyed the affection. I crouched down and rubbed his little brown ears. Mr. Charming had been on my shoulder, but he flew over to his cage in the corner of the room near the front window and perched on the outside arm of it. "Addie's here. Addie's here."

"Don't I wish buddy. Don't I wish."

I set my black Coach tote bag on my old wood dining room table. I loved the worn bag because my Mac fit in it perfectly, but also because it was a gift from my mom when I first signed on to be a ghostwriter with the publisher. It felt like a good luck charm of sorts, and since my mom was gone, I cherished it even more.

I shuffled to the kitchen and prepared a pot of tea. While the water heated, I changed into my pajamas and set up my laptop and story bible on my coffee table. Three years ago, fresh off the marriage bus, I needed a major life change, so I responded to an ad for a ghostwriting job. After submitting copious amounts of writing samples, B.K. Black and her publisher contracted me to write a witch cozy mystery series, and a new witch came to town. A new witch I'd created from my very colorful imagination.

Esmerelda Attlemeyer, the powerful and chosen witch in the magical town of Ascot, was one hundred percent my creation, but I took no credit publicly for her magical adventures or her USA Today bestselling tag. I didn't want the notoriety, and I had no desire to be that public persona social media required of authors. I just wanted to make a living writing. Esmerelda gave me that.

Six books later, and without an end in sight, Esmerelda's recent adventure—solving the murder of a town's favorite witch committed by a horrendous shapeshifter—needed to be written. My heart just wasn't in it.

I wrapped a blanket around me and sipped my hot tea. Cooper's spot on my lap was blocked with my laptop, so he squished himself between my thigh and the side of the couch. Thankfully the pillows were attached, and he couldn't sink into the crack. He liked small spaces, but he shed like an old man going bald, which is exactly why I got that kind of couch in the first place. The thought of his kitty hair piling up between the pillow and the arm of the chair made my stomach hurt.

I stared at the last thing I'd written in Esmerelda's story.

Iris Wolfsbane crossed the room and gazed at the dead witch in the coffin. "This would have never happened if she'd only known how powerful she was."

Dauphin walked over, resting his bony hand on his wife's back. "She was old, her powers weak. She couldn't have stopped it. It was her time."

Esmerelda stepped next to the coffin and placed her hand on Iris's. "I'm so sorry for your loss. She was an astounding witch."

Iris dabbed a tissue to the corner of her eye. "Please, Esmerelda, please help us find the shifter. He must be brought to justice for this."

Esmerelda sighed, her heart breaking for the poor woman. "I'll do what I can, Iris. I promise."

The writing world has two basic types of writers–those that outline their story, and like me, those that fly by the seat of their pants, or, as my editor liked to call it, wing it. Staring at the screen, I wished I was an outliner and not a pantser because I had no idea what happened next. Usually my fingers just hit the keys and my muse popped out and did her thing, but I couldn't even get my fingers to the keyboard let alone find my muse. She'd probably gone on vacation or run away.

I shut the laptop and placed it back on the coffee table. Cooper crawled onto my lap and nuzzled in for another round of snoozing while I flipped through movies on Netflix. Mr. Charming sat on his perch picking at his feathers. I settled on a Christmas romance, something like the Hallmark movies everyone loved. I wasn't big on romance movies like before my divorce, but I hoped once the scars of my failed short marriage faded, I'd enjoy them again. Sometime between the almost first kiss and the dreaded misunderstanding, I shut it off and went to bed, the quiet of the night creeping in through the cracks of my blinds.

I lived on Starlight Street in an apartment on top of The Enchanted. Writing is a lonely job, and if I didn't write at the small bookstore combination coffee shop Bessie owned, I'd probably never see a soul. Holiday Hills residents started their days early, and The Enchanted opened at the crack of dawn. Bessie prepared for her day warming pastries and stocking the small kitchen with sandwich toppings. She once told me she liked getting there early, loved preparing to fill her customers cups with coffee, tea, or hot cocoa, and their bellies with a biscuit or pastry.

The sounds from the kitchen vibrated up and into my bedroom early each morning like clockwork, but I didn't mind. I considered it my own personal alarm, even though I'd gone old school and bought a clock radio for next to my bed. Okay, in my defense, I bought it because it had a charging station on it, and I got tired of digging under my bed to find my phone charger every morning, but it had, a time or two, rescued me from over-sleeping.

I tried hard to sleep through the night, but my nose wouldn't stop running, and I had to begrudgingly drag myself from bed to the bathroom to blow it until after the sixth time, I finally grabbed the roll of toilet paper from the wall and took it to bed with me.

I didn't need that alarm the next morning. Poor Mr. Charming missed his momma, something I understood completely, and chattered away before sunrise. It was a good thing too because that brand-new clock radio flashed twelve o'clock instead of the actual time. Either it was broken, or I'd had a power surge. I crawled underneath my bed to make sure Cooper hadn't messed with the cord. He liked to pull it out and bat it around. It was still plugged into the power outlet.

Cooper stood and stretched. I followed suit, but only with the stretching part. Warm and comfy back under my soft down comforter, I wasn't quite ready to venture out of bed and start my day.

* * *

Mr. Charming flew from my arm and over to the three men sitting on the old leather chairs in the front corner of The Enchanted. He perched on his regular spot, Merlock Dupe's chairback, his favorite. "Time for coffee. Time for coffee."

"Hello parrot," Merlock said. "Again."

I caught the eye of Peter Parallel, the least grouchy of them, and he chuckled as he nodded toward Merlock. "That parrot has a crush on you, old man."

Merlock grunted as Mr. Charming picked at his hair. "Knock it off parrot."

Cooper jumped into the display area and snuggled into a ball on the antique cloth chair, giving Bessie a little live front window display. She always decorated the old-fashioned window for the holidays and Cooper would bring life to the display, sort of. He'd sleep, but the snoring would alert people to his beating heart.

Bessie handed me a cup of coffee. "It's a new blend I'm playing with. Let me know what you think."

A memory flashed through my mind. When Mom retired from her job at the hospital, she started helping Bessie. It wasn't intentional, she was just there so often, Bessie finally gave her a paycheck. That first time Bessie slapped the check in my mother's hand, they'd argued about it. Mom tossed the check back at her friend and ran toward the back of the store.

"You aren't paying me a dime, old woman," she hollered.

Bessie chased after her, waving the check in her hand and yelling, "You'll take it and you'll like it, old woman!"

I laughed. Mom swore she'd never take money to help a friend, but Bessie kept writing those checks. I smiled the other day when I found them in a zip lock bag in her kitchen desk. She hadn't cashed a single one.

While working for Bessie, the two of them became coffee aficionados of sorts, creating unique blends from bean combinations they discovered on the internet. I never much paid attention to how they did it, but every time Bessie had a new blend, I loved it.

The door to the store opened and the loud bell attached to it dinged.

Merlock covered his ears. "Criminy, I hate that thing."

"Oh hush," Bessie said. She greeted the police chief with a

toothy smile and a hug. "Hey there handsome, you want your regular today?" She flipped around and headed to the counter.

He removed his hat. "Yes, ma'am."

Bessie stopped in her tracks. "If I've told you once, I've told you a thousand times, it's Bessie."

"Yes, ma—Bessie."

She winked at him. "Better."

When she poured his coffee, little sparkles appeared over the cup. I shook my head and they disappeared. "Weird." Maybe Stella was right. Maybe I did need to chill.

"What's weird honey?" she asked.

"Oh, nothing. I just thought I saw something, but I didn't."

Chief Ryder caught my eye and smiled. Every time he did that little butterflies took flight in my stomach. I'd secretly crush on the man when visiting Holiday Hills, even before Zachary cheated on me and packed his things to shack up with the other woman in the city. When I moved back to town, seeing Chief Ryder daily did nothing to lessen the crush.

Pretty much every woman in Holiday Hills had a crush on Gabe Ryder. In a town of less than 10,000, eligible bachelors were slim pickings, and most of the ones available resembled Santa Claus or the dorky sidekick cop in 80s police dramas. Not the police chief though. He wasn't from Holiday Hills, and it showed.

The mayor hired Chief Ryder a few years ago when Old Chief Bruster retired. Crime wasn't a thing in Holiday Hills, but the town still needed a chief. From what I'd heard, Gabe Ryder left a big detective job in Atlanta hoping for a quieter life in a small town. I didn't know the specific details, but apparently his wife was killed by someone he'd arrested. It was probably easier for him to deal with the loss if he didn't have to stare it directly in the face.

Every woman in town flaunted herself around the tall blond hottie, but none of them broke through his shell.

He towered over me sitting at my table. "I'm sorry about your mom. She was a nice woman."

I stood and was just a few inches shorter than him. "Thank you." Something tickled the inside of my nose, but I didn't dare rub it. One never knew what could accidentally slip out, and I didn't want to embarrass myself around him.

"You doing okay?"

I gripped my fingers together behind my back and rocked onto the heels of my brown boots. I did that when I was nervous, and Chief Ryder made me nervous. "Yeah, I'm...I'm getting there."

My nose itched, and I carefully, and hopefully quietly, breathed in through it to make it stop.

It didn't work.

It caught his attention, and I watched his eyebrow twitch upward as he stared at the middle of my face. I couldn't help it, I had to scratch the darn itch.

A small display of journals Bessie had stacked on the counter dropped onto the ground. Chief Ryder whipped around, and Bessie rushed to clean them.

I rubbed at my nose again to make sure nothing had slipped out, and another pile of journals spilled to the ground.

"Oh dear, must have knocked them when I moved the candies. My bad," Bessie said.

The chief offered her a single nod and then faced me again. "Yes, well, it takes time."

I caught Bessie eyeing me suspiciously.

"Time. Yes, I'm sure you would—I mean, yes. Time. It takes time."

He smiled. "Speaking of time, I need to get to work. Got to keep the streets free of crime and all that."

"Yeah." I pointed my finger in the air. "And you're doing a great job of that."

Bessie moved to behind the counter and covered a grin.

When the door shut, and the chief was out of sight, I fell back into my seat and groaned. "I sounded like the biggest idiot ever."

Bessie full out laughed that time. "Oh sweetie, I could cut the tension with a knife between the two of you." She topped off my coffee with a splash of some from a fresh pot. "Looks like someone has a crush."

"Ugh, was I that obvious?"

"I'm not talking about you, sugar."

* * *

Esmerelda stepped back and wiggled herself behind the cement support wall of the bridge. She braced herself as the ground vibrated beneath her. The shifter was close, she could feel him, smell him even. She pressed her back against the cold cement, willing herself to be as small as possible. She squeezed her eyes shut and pictured a small fire ant, and without a spark, turned herself into the tiny creature crawling up the wall.

The shifter rushed through the trees and stopped short at the bridge, his beady wolf eyes scrutinizing the area. He dipped his head to the ground and sniffed, following the scent of the witch to the cement wall.

His nose landed just an inch below the fire ant, and Esmerelda scurried up the wall and into a groove of the cement, her little ant body anxious and nervous.

Shifters and witches feuded like the Hatfield's and McCoy's, and if a shifter caught a witch, that witch disappeared forever.

I hit save and closed the document. Sometimes, when I didn't know what to write next in the story, I'd skip to another section and write in it. Eventually I'd have to combine the sections, and matching them up took some effort, but it helped my muse do her thing.

Bessie fixed a dish full of chopped fruit and veggies for Mr. Charming and he picked at them on my table. His little moaning sounds while he ate made me smile. The day sailed by quickly, and I'd actually managed to get seven thousand words written. I credited that to the fact that Stella had to go to the city to meet with her author. Stella was a freelance editor, and she'd made a living editing horror fiction. The thrill of that genre was lost on me, but she enjoyed it, and she was known to be one of the best in her field. I read some of what I'd written. It wasn't award winning, but every author knew bad words were better than no words, so at least there was that. I'd edit through them before sending the manuscript off to the editor at the publisher anyway.

I stretched and let out a soft groan as I cleaned up my things. It felt good to move around. Sitting and writing in the zone can be hard on the bones, even for someone my age. I walked over to Bessie at the opposite end of the store. "Can you keep Mr. Charming here for a bit? I'd like to run a quick errand."

"Honey, you know that parrot practically lives here. You go on and do what you need to do. If you need me to keep him for the night, just let me know. He loves his sleepovers with his Auntie Bessie."

"Thanks, I may take you up on that."

I drove over to the Holiday Hills Cemetery where the Odell family tomb is located, and where my mother's remains were laid to rest the day before. Mr. Remington said they'd intern her remains the day of her life celebration, and I wanted to go by and if nothing, touch the marble closing her into the tomb.

My mom took me to the cemetery a lot as a child. I'd never met any of my family, they'd all died before I was born, including my father. But family history was important to my mom. Our ancestors, she'd always said, shaped our future, and it was important to keep them alive in our hearts.

We'd visit once every few weeks and she'd tell me a story about someone, maybe my uncle Adrian or one of my grandparents. All in all, there were twenty-seven Odell's interned in that tomb, and most of them from over a hundred years ago. I took comfort in knowing my mother wasn't alone in her final resting place. I tried to remind myself that I wasn't alone either, but having no biological family alive anymore made that hard.

Holiday Hills cemetery sat on the outskirts of the western part of town, near Route 369. There were several quick routes to get to it, but I preferred the long drive through the outskirts of town. North Georgia rested at the start of the Appalachian Mountains, and the mountain roads followed the paths created by the loggers and gold miners from years ago. I loved the curvy twists and turns through the mountains, enjoyed the wooded scenery and small farms dotting the land along the way.

At least once a month my mother and I would have to pull to the side of the road and coax a cow, horse, or pig to the side. Horses and pigs were easy, but the cows required a certain skill —one my mom had, and I didn't.

Huntington Holiday, the town's founder, gave one hundred acres of his land to build the cemetery, but did so on one condition. He required only residents of town be buried there. Most people didn't mind, but I thought the rule was outdated and unfair. What if, for example, Zach and I had children? We moved to his hometown, Cumming Georgia, a few days after our honeymoon. If we'd have stayed together and had kids—an alarming thought given his selfish nature—and stayed in Cumming, those children couldn't be buried in Holiday Hills. I shuddered at the thought, though I wasn't sure which one, having kids with Zach, or their burial location.

Huntington Holiday created a town constitution and many of the rules were antiquated and outdated, but the town itself believed in staying true to the founder's vision.

I pulled up to the wrought iron gate and climbed out of my car to open it. A light breeze whipped over me and sent a chill shivering through my body. The gate was never locked, but it stayed closed. The gate's ornate design, a lion's head on each side, looked nice with it closed. I didn't have to unlatch the handle, which, in retrospect was odd, but at the time, I didn't think much of it. My fingers were stiff from the cold, and all I cared about was running back to the car to slip on my pea coat before driving out to the tomb. It didn't normally get below forty-five during the day in our northern part of the state, but the past week we'd barely made it over forty. I didn't have a warm enough jacket for that kind of weather.

I drove through the gate and jumped back out to close it, making sure to secure the latch from both sides.

I loved driving through the cemetery. Since I'd been going from an early age, I felt comfortable there. A sense of peace surrounded me, and I always felt like the people buried there were happy to have visitors, whether they were there for them or not. It sounded silly, but it was a heck of a lot better than how Stella felt every time she went with me. Stella believed in ghosts and was on edge every time we went. One poke of my finger on her shoulder sent her into a round of girly horror movie-like screams.

So I did it all the time. Who wouldn't?

Most of the Odell family tomb was public, meaning a person could walk through it. The original tomb, one made with marble granite from Ball Ground, Georgia, remained closed and private. The addition built in the mid-1900s though was open and anyone could walk around it. The design wouldn't win any architectural awards, but if one liked a mix of early 1800s granite and stone design blended with the mid-1900s trend, it worked. My mother loved the quirkiness of its appearance, and I'd grown to appreciate it, too.

The winding road to the family tomb took me the length of the cemetery out to the far left corner. Along the way I passed the Holiday family tomb and several other prominent family's resting places. Sun blanched angels and towering statues of men and women flanked old, dried up gardens surrounding some of the graves. Once spring came, residents would come and clean up the gardens, some planting new flowers for their loved ones.

I knew many of the people interned inside that fence, and I understood that as time passed, I'd know even more.

I parked my car off the side of the road and shimmied into my light winter jacket. I kept a pair of mittens in my glove compartment and searched through the mess of previous oil change papers and tire rotations until I found them. Unlike the rest of my things, the tight compartment was a mess, and I reminded myself to clean it out when I got home.

Cooper caught a glimpse of me leaving The Enchanted and after a long, meow-filled stretch, had followed behind me. He sat nuzzled in the passenger's seat snoring, so I left him there. I kissed the top of his forehead and whispered, "Be right back little guy."

The cold air of the evening wisped around me, settling deep within my bones. Light rain headed our direction, and at that time of year, since we rarely got the full-blown thunderstorms like in the spring, with our height in the mountains, it would more than likely turn to snow. I didn't mind. We got a few inches of the white stuff every year, and though it closed down most towns around us, mine stayed open. Since Holiday Hills was so small, some of our store owners walked to their stores and opened for business during what the weather reporters always called a winter storm. I could always get a cup of coffee and a pastry at The Enchanted or a traditional southern breakfast from the Corner Café.

I rubbed my arms, regretting that I hadn't brought a warmer jacket or at least added a few layers of clothing before heading to the cemetery. As always, I said a silent hello to the people buried in the area of the path to our tomb, thinking about their lives and wondering how they lived. I didn't know any of them, but my mother told me stories about some.

The tomb had three small walkways; one bordering the front, another splitting it into two sections down the middle, and a final one bordering the back. The last one had a small path of maybe three feet that led to the original tomb. Everything was covered with a trellis that, in the spring, had the most beautiful yellow flowering vine blooming on it.

My mother's final resting place was on that back side, next to her parents and grandparents. Below them were three empty spots I knew had been left for my family. Three spots for two children and myself, or, if I married again, which was highly unlikely, a spot for my husband, a child, and myself. I brushed the thought off as I walked the short distance through the family tomb, knowing it was the last thing I needed to think about.

I ran my hand across a few name plates, retelling bits of their stories to myself as I did. The Odell family owned a big piece of colorful history in Holiday Hills, and I always smiled as I walked through the tomb thinking about the things my mother shared throughout the years.

My great uncle Ayden, for example, considered himself a spiritual insight. I'd never quite figured out what that meant, but my mother claimed he used crystals to tell the future and help people make decisions in their lives. She said the crystals were a direct connection to his spirit guides, which, the family believed, were deceased Odell's. Great Uncle Adyen died when I was a baby, but he'd told my mom I would live a long, happy life, have an amazing, loving husband and one child. If my past was any indication of the truth behind my great uncle's abilities, he must have been a charlatan.

And he would have predicted the dead woman lying in a puddle of blood below my mother's remains.

CHAPTER 2

$\mathcal{I}$ rushed over to the woman. "Hello? Ma'am?"

What was I thinking? Hello, ma'am? As if a deceased woman could answer me. I didn't know what to do. I crouched down, moved her long gray hair away from her neck, and checked for a pulse. Nothing. I stood and turned in circles. "Hello? Is anyone here?" I backed up and pressed my body against the tomb's cold marble to keep a tight view on my surroundings. I pulled my cell phone out of my pocket and dialed 911.

It took the police less than five minutes to arrive, but the ambulance took a little longer. We didn't have a full-time fire department, and that included the EMTs.

The 911 operator had me step back from the body, which I'd already done, but I kept her in my line of sight, just in case.

When Chief Ryder pulled up, I bolted to his car, my breathing shallow and quick. "She's…there's…"

He placed his hand on my shoulder. "Abby, breath. It's going to be okay."

Sure, said the guy who'd probably seen a hundred dead bodies before. She was my first, at least the kind that hadn't already been placed in a coffin, and I planned on that being my only one.

Cooper rubbed against my ankles. I glanced down at him, wondering how he'd gotten out of my car. I took two deep breaths.

Chief Ryder kept his eyes focused on mine. "Better?"

I nodded. Cooper continued to do a crazy eight through my legs and added some seriously intense meowing. I picked him up, and he crawled high enough on my chest to burrow his head into my neck. His warm head and regulated breathing comforted me.

"Okay, can you tell me what happened?"

I pointed to the woman's body with my free hand. "I walked over to my mom's, you know, and she was there, on the ground. I…I checked for a pulse, but I couldn't find one. I'm pretty sure she's dead."

"It appears that way." He removed a small notepad and pen from his shirt pocket. "What time did you find her?"

"Right when I called 911, so maybe, I don't know, ten minutes ago. Give or take."

He cleared his throat. "Do you know her?"

"No, but I think she was at my mom's celebration of life."

"You *think?*"

"Well, I mean, she's wearing the same long black dress, and I'm pretty sure that's her hair, but I only saw the woman briefly, and to be honest, I didn't see the back of her head. I'd need to see her face to make sure."

"I think we can probably arrange that."

"There's a lot of blood."

He nodded. "Yes."

"Do you know what happened?"

"How about you sit tight for a few minutes? I've got to take care of some things, but I'll be back to check on you in a bit, okay?"

I nodded.

As he walked away, he called over to a paramedic. "Jimmy, get Ms. Odell a blanket, will you?

The paramedic strongly suggested I sit in the ambulance because I was shivering, and my teeth chattered beyond my control. "Let's keep you warm." He whispered to the other paramedic. "Looks like a mild case of shock going on, can you attend to her? I'm going to help Ryder."

"Got it," the other guy said.

I didn't feel like I was in shock. I just felt cold. And sad. And confused.

Another car pulled up to the family tomb and parked. A large —and by large, I meant round—older man, with a balding head stepped out. I'd never seen him before, so he couldn't have been from town.

Chief Ryder approached him, and the two shook hands.

"Abby."

"Yes?"

The paramedic turned toward me. "Yes, ma'am?"

"You said my name."

He furrowed his brow. "Wasn't me."

I pressed my lips together. "Oh, I'm sorry. I thought I heard my name."

He smiled and stepped out of the ambulance. "You stay put. We'll be back to check on you in a bit."

"Okay."

Cooper crawled off my lap and stood at the edge of the ambulance, peeking out at his surroundings.

"Abby."

I leaned forward, and Cooper hissed. He'd heard it too. I tossed the blanket off my shoulders and walked with my shoulders crouched to the edge of the ambulance and stared outside. There were several people around, but none close to me.

"Abby."

Cooper hissed again. I jumped out of the ambulance and

grabbed my cat. "It's okay little guy. It's probably just someone over there."

I carried him to the small crowd of city employees surrounding the woman's body. When one stepped away, I caught a glimpse of her. Someone turned her over, and that's when I knew for sure it was the woman from the funeral home. I stood there with my mouth hanging open, staring, when suddenly a burst of cold air hit me. Cooper wrapped his little front legs around my neck, flipped his head into the cold air and hissed.

"It's okay," I said, patting him on the head.

The cold air settled around me, and a foggy cloud shaped into a dark form before me.

"It's coming for you, Abby."

Cooper hissed again. My jaw dropped, and everything went black.

* * *

"She's waking up," Bessie said.

"Oh, thank God," Stella said.

My right hand hurt like the dickens. I tried to move it, but a pain shot through it and up my arm. "Ouch." I opened my eyes to see Bessie and Stella hovered over me.

I blinked as I examined the unfamiliar room. The sterile pale yellow walls were empty other than a small flat screen TV, a white board with scribblings I couldn't make out, a round numbered clock, and a poster with cookies above numbers. I squinted, trying to figure out what it was. "Is that a pain chart? With cookies on it?"

Stella laughed. "Yup."

The fluorescent light above me made my eyes hurt, and the consistent, shrill sounding beeping sound from a monitor on my right attached itself to my mind, forcing me to think in rhythm. "That. Beeping. Is. Annoying."

"Well hello there, sweetie," Bessie said. "Glad your happy self could make it to the party."

Stella smiled so big I saw the beginnng of her molars. "You scared the molasses out of us."

Something else beeped next to me, the rhythm slightly different than the other beep. "Am I in the hospital?" I rubbed my horribly dry and crusty eyes and a shooting pain seared through my temples. I pinched my nostrils. "What—"

A man screamed, "The president was—"

I winced, pulling my shoulders up next to my head. "Oh, that hurts."

The man stopping screaming.

"Sorry about that," Bessie said. "I must have hit the TV remote on accident."

Things came back to me in bits and pieces. The cemetery. The woman on the ground. The blood. Chief Ryder. Someone whispering my name, and finally, a skinny pole of a nurse telling me this might hurt a bit then sticking a knitting needle into the back of my hand. "What happened?"

"You fell and hit your head," Stella said.

I tried to sit up, but my head throbbed with the effort. "Ow."

"Here, let me help you." She pressed a button on the side of the bed and it sat me up. "Better?"

"Yeah, thanks."

"You've got a pretty serious bump going on. I bet your head hurts something awful."

"Here. If it's bad, press this button," Bessie said. She handed me a remote control. "It's pain medicine."

I pressed the button, and the TV blasted on again, the same man talking about the president.

"Whoops." She yanked the remote from my hand. "That's the TV remote. Sorry."

Stella handed me another small clicker type thing. "It's this one."

"I'm fine." I didn't want any pain medicine. I was groggy enough, and I wanted to be clear when I headed home.

"The good news is you're going to be fine." Stella tucked the thin white blanket up under my side. "The bad news is you have to eat hospital food for breakfast."

"Breakfast?"

She nodded. "You've been sleeping like a baby all night."

"Cooper." I felt like someone had stuffed an entire bag of cotton in my mouth and left it there while I slept. "May I have some water, please?"

"Of course." Stella handed me a water bottle with a long plastic bendy straw that had been sitting on a table attached to my bed. "You've got all the fancy fixings here."

"Looks like it." I sipped the cold, refreshing water and let some sit in my mouth. When I swallowed it, I felt the coldness travel down my throat. It was heavenly. "Where's Cooper?"

"He stayed the night at my place," Bessie said. "He's probably torturing Mr. Charming while we speak."

I laughed. "Probably." I took another sip of water. By far, it was the best tasting stuff I'd ever had. "What time is it?"

Stella pointed to a clock on the wall in front of us. "Just after nine." Her eyes widened. "Oh crap. I have to go. I've got a conference call with my author at nine thirty." She bent toward me and kissed me on the forehead. "Unless you don't behave, you'll be out of hospital jail in a few hours. I'll come back and get you."

"It's okay," Bessie said, waving Stella off. "I've got her. You go work."

"But The Enchanted," I said. "You need to be there." Bessie was an employee down since my mother died, which left her as her only employee. You need to open."

"The Enchanted can wait. You're more important than that silly old bookstore."

"It serves coffee and pastries, too."

She chuckled and her chubby cheeks shook. "Don't you worry. We have some things to discuss now anyway."

Stella left and another woman walked in. "Look at you, all awake and chatty." The petite nurse's blue eyes shined, highlighting her olive skin, and her long black hair made the green drab scrubs brighter too. She removed a clipboard from the foot of my bed, flipped through the pages, and then fussed with the annoying beeping thing on my side.

I held up my aching hand. "Did you do this to me?"

A smile filled her face. "I did not, but I'm the one that's taking it out for you."

"Is that going to hurt?"

She shrugged and carefully picked up my hand. "Whoever did that job needs a refresher course. You're going to have a big bruise."

"Great. It'll be like a tan."

Chief Ryder stepped quietly into the room and cleared his throat.

Bessie walked over and gave him a hug. "Chief."

"Bessie, may I have a moment with Ms. Odell, please?"

She crooked her head to the side. "Of course. I'll be out here."

The nurse finished applying a band aid to my hand. "The doctor will be in to sign your release papers in a bit."

"So, I'm leaving?"

"Barring any unforeseen circumstances, yes."

I didn't want to know what those could be, so I just smiled and said thank you.

She closed the door behind her.

Chief Ryder came closer and towered over me. I hated being below people. I'd spent most of my life above them, and below felt so awkward. "How are you feeling?"

"I have a headache."

"I can understand that. You hit the ground pretty hard."

"Did you see?"

He nodded.

"What happened?"

"I was going to ask you the same question."

"I don't know. I mean, one minute I'm at the cemetery and the next I'm lying here with a doozy of a headache."

"Minor concussion. The doctor wanted to keep you over night because your blood pressure dropped pretty low."

"How do you know that?"

He shrugged. "I've got connections." The side of his mouth twitched.

"Well, I'm sure it's fine now or they wouldn't be letting me out but thank you for checking on me."

"Actually, that's only part of the reason I'm here."

I raised an eyebrow.

"The woman you found. You said you didn't know her, correct?"

I nodded.

"You sure? Maybe when you were a kid or something?"

I shook my head.

"Ever seen any photos of her, like in a family album?"

"No. Why?"

"Did you meet any of your mother's siblings?"

"No. Her family's dead. She lost her brother Adrian before I was born."

"The woman you found yesterday is Allegra Odell. Your mother's sister."

I blinked. "Excuse me?"

He inhaled and released the breath slowly. "According to her ID and a quick check of birth records. We're running a dental check just to verify, but I thought you should know."

"I honestly—I...it's not possible. If my mother had a sister, she would have told me."

"I can't explain any of that. I just know what we discovered in our identification process."

I couldn't even begin to imagine my mother having a sister and keeping it from me. It made no sense. "How did she die?"

"She was shot."

My eyes widened, and my head pounded. I had an aunt, an aunt that was murdered.

Chief Ryder gave me a moment and then he spoke. "I wanted to make sure you knew before word got out."

"Yeah, thanks. I appreciate that. What uh, what happens now?"

"This is a homicide. We're investigating."

"Yeah, I know. I mean, with her uh, remains."

"She'll be released after an autopsy, and then you'll be able to—"

I cut him off. "Okay, and the investigation?"

"I'll keep you informed, Ms. Odell."

"Thank you." He nodded and moved toward the hospital room door.

"Chief Ryder?"

He turned around. "Yes?"

"Could you call me Abby?"

He smiled. "Abby it is."

* * *

After a stern talking to about following my release orders she'd handed me, a Nurse Ratched type nurse wheeled me down to the hospital entrance. She reminded me of my third-grade teacher, an old lady with a granny bun, a closet full of house dresses, and a scary personality. I knew better than to argue with either of them.

Bessie waited outside and helped me out of the chair. Nurse Ratched reviewed my prescription directions one more time, encouraged me to get more rest, and bid us goodbye.

Bessie started her car. "Let's hope that woman's not a grandmother."

I chewed on my bottom lip.

"How're you feeling?"

I stared out the front window as she drove toward town.

"Sweetie?"

"Did you know my mother had a sister?"

She blew out a breath. "Let's get you settled first and then we'll have a chat."

I took a quick shower, scrubbed the sterile bleachy smell of the hospital from my skin, and wrapped my hair in a towel.

Bessie propped me up on my couch, stuffed a pillow behind my back, and tucked a warm throw around my legs. "I've got a pot of tea on. Are you hungry? I can make you something."

"No, thank you. Can we talk now?"

"Let me just get your tea and then I'll run home and pick up Cooper and Mr. Charming. Then we can talk, okay?"

My nose itched. I felt a sneeze coming and looked toward the window to let the sun encourage it, but it wasn't all that sunny out. The sneeze escaped anyway, and I rubbed my nose.

My Amazon Echo flipped on and the Eagles "Lying Eyes" played.

Bessie coughed. "The electrical wiring in this building is just awful." She rushed to the small round Echo on a shelf across the room and poked her finger on it, but the music didn't stop. "We've been having a time with it downstairs."

"Alexa, shut off the music," I said.

The Echo went silent.

Bessie's eyes widened. "When did you start doing that?"

"Doing what?"

"Commanding things."

I laughed. "It's what you're supposed to do with Alexa. She's like an electronic, I don't know, entertainment system or something. There's a name for it, but my head hurts too much to think that hard."

Her eyes shifted from the Dot to me. "Technology makes no sense to me."

"You're not the only one. I'm a millennial and I still don't get some of it."

She walked into the kitchen and reappeared with a cup of hot tea. "There, this should keep you until I'm back. We can talk then."

"Bessie, wait. What's going on?"

"What do you mean?"

"You're avoiding the subject."

"Avoiding? I'm not avoiding anything. I just want everything settled first."

"Why?"

She stood over me and groaned. "I don't know why she didn't do this before. I told her to."

I scooted further up onto the side of the couch. "What're you talking about? Please. I don't know what's going on, but Chief Ryder said the woman I found is my aunt, and she was murdered. I didn't even know I had an aunt."

She bit her fingernail.

"Please, Bessie, tell me what's going on."

She exhaled and plopped down onto the couch beside me. "I'll tell you everything, I promise, but I need to get something first, okay? It'll help you understand."

My head pounded. I closed my eyes and burrowed myself into the back of the couch. "Okay. I'm a little tired at the moment anyway."

I woke up several hours later to a toasty silky brick of a cat snoozing on my lap and a singing parrot on his perch in the corner of the room. Bessie had left the building, or at least my apartment's portion of it. My body ached but my head hurt less than earlier, so I considered that a win. I carefully slid my hands under Cooper's little body and moved him in one big heap onto the couch next to me. He didn't bother waking up. As I walked into my bedroom, I stepped on a pile of dirty laundry I'd been avoiding and decided a mild concussion was the perfect excuse to let the dry cleaners handle it all. I splashed some water on my face and patted it dry.

My Echo exploded to life again in my family room, this time playing the Eagles version of "Please Come Home for Christmas". Bessie really needed to get those circuits looked at. "Alexa, stop the music."

The music stopped, but it had awakened Cooper, who glared at me with one eye when I walked past the couch. "Hey, it's not my fault. Talk to Bessie about it."

I headed to the kitchen for a glass of water, but I could have sworn I heard someone whisper *"whatever"*. I chalked it up to a bump on my head and a large dose of medicine. Medicine always left me feeling like a fraternity pledge after a long night of drinking.

I searched the kitchen for my cell phone and found it plugged into the charger with a note underneath it.

You've got a sandwich and a bag of chips in a lunch bag on the counter. I cut up some veggies and fruit for Mr. Charming. They're in the 'fridge. Cooper's been fed. You should be good for the night. I'll see you in the morning. Call if you need anything. Love you, Bessie.

Oh, no. No, no, no. She wasn't getting off that easy. I unplugged my phone, grabbed the bag with the food and headed back to the couch. "Siri, call Bessie."

"Which number, work or home?"

"Work."

"Calling Bessie Durham work."

It went to her answering machine. Bessie was old school. "Hello. You've reached The Enchanted. We are currently closed. Please leave a message at the beep, and we'll get back to you during open hours."

I hung up. A quick glance at the clock showed me it was after ten o'clock. The Enchanted would be closed. I couldn't believe I'd slept that long. I must have really needed the rest. I knew Bessie would be asleep already, and I assumed she'd come by earlier, found me sleeping, made me the food, and then left quietly. I felt bad for thinking she had tried to avoid our talk when really she just wanted to let me rest.

I set the bag of food on my coffee table next to an envelope with my mother's handwriting. For Abigail, it said. Bessie must have left it for me. I held the envelope up to my face and smelled my mother's favorite perfume, Poison, by Christian Dior. I closed my eyes and soaked in the smell, letting the memories of my mom fill my head and my heart. Cooper moved onto the top of the blanket and onto the pillow shoved into the crook of the couch. I gently lifted him, sat down, pulled the blanket back over my legs, and set him on my lap. He purred softly and went right back to sleep. I kissed the envelope and opened it carefully.

Dear Abigail,

If you're reading this, it means I've left you sooner than I expected, and I am so very sorry. The last thing I ever wanted to do was leave you without telling you the truth in person. I hope you will forgive me.

There are so many things you don't know, so many things I didn't get to tell you, and many of them won't make a lick of sense. I just ask that you trust me, trust Bessie, and know I only wanted what was best for you.

She will explain, and she will help you through this new experience. Listen to her, do what she says, and you will be just fine.

Know, sweetheart, that I am not gone. I am with you always, and I will be there if you need me. I am just a heartbeat away.

My love for you is beyond description, and that is why I did what I did.

Mom

I stared at the handwritten letter, tears flowing down my cheeks and landing on Cooper's head. He lifted his head, gave me a one-eyed glare, and went back to sleep.

I wiped my cheeks with the sleeve of my sweatshirt and scratched my nose. My TV booted on and went straight to the

Rokú home screen. I groaned, losing patience with Bessie's electricity issue.

I searched the table for the remote, but it wasn't there. I often left it on the couch and I had a feeling it was nestled between the cushions beneath me. I wiggled around, hoping to feel it or jar it loose, waking Cooper up in the process. Instead of his typical one-eyed glare, he pushed himself up, stretched, and then glared at me with both eyes.

"I'm sorry. I can't find the remote. I can't just say TV off and—"

The TV shut off.

I stared at Cooper, then the TV, and then back to Cooper. I pressed my lips together. "It's the electricity. Bessie needs to have it checked." It wasn't because my mother hadn't been hallucinating and talking crazy talk the night she'd died. Nope. Wasn't that. Couldn't have been that.

Or could it?

I shook my head, the insane thoughts just beating the bellows of my brain instead of emptying out through my ears.

Cooper didn't seem to care much about anything I said. He just wanted to find a new comfortable spot that let him snooze in peace. He stretched his way to the other side of the couch and went back to that place most cats spent the good portion of their lives.

I found the remote stuck between the couch cushions and clicked on the TV, but nothing happened. I groaned in frustration. I stared at the letter. I groaned some more. I stared at the TV. Neither were things I wanted to deal with, nor were they things I understood at that moment.

Stella's biggest complaint about me was my ability to shove things under the rug. If I pretended there wasn't a problem, there wasn't a problem. She thought that was ridiculous and repeatedly got on my case about it. Zach's affair was an excellent example. For months I knew he was cheating on me. I sensed it in his actions, the way he no longer snuggled his back against mine in the middle of the night, the way his eyes no longer crinkled at the sides when he smiled at me wearing his button down business shirts he'd asked me to take to the dry cleaners the day before. But I wasn't ready to deal with it, and until I could, I just pretended he wasn't. Stella, on the other hand, wore her emotions on her sleeve, as my mother used to say. When she felt something, all of Holiday Hills knew it. Happy Stella made the world a brighter, better place, but steaming Stella—my nickname for her when she was angry—was a time bomb ready to explode, and it usually did.

Steaming Stella hammered the final nail in the coffin of my marriage. I was upset then, but looking back, I knew she'd done me a favor. Like having to deal with Zach's infidelity, I also knew that eventually I'd have to deal with the letter. My mother wouldn't have been ominous about something trivial, and she wouldn't have brought Bessie into it if it wasn't important. But that night I just wanted to bask in the comfort of my cozy home, the murmured humming of my parrot sibling, and the soft rhythmic snoring of my devoted kitty.

* * *

Merlock Dupe leaned toward Peter Parallel and jabbed his finger at the man, his angry eyes so narrowed I couldn't see his pupils. "They might get a bowl, but it'll be one of those stupid ones like the Dry Cleaners Bowl or something. One that don't matter, that's for sure. They haven't had a strong defense all season, and their running back, what's his name? Someone needs to teach that boy how to play the game."

Peter shook his head. "You don't know what you're talking about. They're number one in the SEC." He shook the pages of the newspaper and raised them up to read, covering his face from Merlock in a dismissive manner.

I grinned as I walked past the ever-bickering men. "Morning, gentlemen. Go Dawgs."

Merlock directed his loud grunt at me.

I caught Peter's eye and winked at him. He gave me a sweet smile, the one that showed he's missing an upper tooth on the right side. When Peter smiled his toothy smile, it was because he was genuinely happy. If you didn't get the toothless smile, he wasn't your fan.

Bessie fixed me a cup of coffee while Cooper readied himself for another hard day of rest. Mr. Charming perched behind Merlock, ready and willing to pick at the man's receding hairline until he'd officially drove him crazy. All was good, or as good as it could be considering my mother was dead, and I'd found a dead body lying in the middle of the Odell family tomb.

Bessie said, "How're you doing honey?" She made eye contact but only for a second. Bessie was everyone's friend, and a true southern woman. Stout and strong with a long braid of gray hair touching her waist, she was the kindest woman in town, acted like everyone's grandmother. If you had a cold, you came to Bessie. Had a problem that needed solving, Bessie threw up her *the doctor is in* sign and solved it with you. She looked everyone in the eye when she spoke to them. She didn't avoid subjects. But, on the other hand, if you hurt someone she cared for, all bets were off. Bessie jumped into protective mode, claws out, fangs showing. She'd almost sent Zach to the hospital with a minor glance I'd swore shot daggers from her angry eyes.

Okay, that was an exaggeration. Zach's appendix burst, but the timing of Bessie's disgust and his surgery were so close, Stella joked Bessie caused it. Bessie didn't seem to mind the accusation either.

I took a deep breath, and she patted my hand. "Is it your head still? Maybe you should go back to bed?"

"No, my head is fine. I wanted to talk about the letter you left last night."

She averted her eyes from mine, wiping the small counter and scrubbing an imaginary spot clean. "Now's not the time."

I pulled the envelope out from the waistline of my jeans. "Please?"

She stared at the envelope and then up at me, locking her eyes with mine for a solid few seconds. She sighed, grabbed the pot of French roast coffee, and stepped around the counter. "All right boys, The Enchanted is closed. I'll refill your cups, but you're going to have to argue about football somewhere else this morning."

Peter stretched himself out of the chair, pushing his hips forward once vertical. "Well, you finally did it, old man. I told you all this bickering would wear thin. Now we got to drink our coffee in the cold." He caught my eye for a moment, and I flinched. Something told me he wasn't playing around.

Merlock mumbled something too inappropriate to repeat. "Don't blame it on me. I didn't say nothing bad. Probably just closing to fix the electrical wiring. Darn lights can't seem to stop flickering the past few days."

Bessie made a *tsk* sound and patted Merlock on the back. "This isn't your fault, and my electrical system is fine. I just need some private time with Abby."

Merlock groaned, but the men put on their coats and left. Cooper glanced up briefly from his spot in the window, stretched, and then meandered his way toward my regular spot. Mr. Charming flew over to the counter and perched on top of a pile of used Harlan Coben hardcover books.

Bessie flipped the open sign to closed. "Come on, you need to be sitting down for this." She rubbed Mr. Charming on the head as she walked by.

I dragged my front teeth over my bottom lip. "This is bad isn't it? I'm adopted. That's it. I'm adopted." I dropped into my chair and ran my hand through my hair. "I mean, I should have known. We're nothing alike, complete opposites actually. How did I not see this before?"

"Good grief, child." She sat next to me and patted my knee. "You're an Odell through and through."

I didn't really think I was adopted. I had my mother's eyes, though hers were softer, filled with a life of adventure and experience.

Cooper jumped onto the empty chair and then propelled himself onto the table. He sat in front of me, his dark eyes burrowing into mine. I picked him up and put him on my lap, but he crawled up my chest and positioned his head in its regular spot, the crook of my neck. It gave me comfort for what I expected would be something horrible. I didn't want to cry. When the lump in my throat formed, I swallowed it back, and I blinked away the tears, rubbing my cheek into my cat's soft fur. I scratched my nose to stop from sniffling. Cooper nuzzled his face deeper into my neck.

The lights flickered, and Bessie smiled. "You'll get a handle on that soon."

I blinked. "I'll get a handle on what?"

She smiled. "The electricity. It'll just take some practice, but I'll help you with that."

"What?"

She patted my leg again and brushed a strand of hair from my face. "Your mother wanted you to have a normal childhood. She planned to tell you everything when the time was right, but she got sick."

My eyes widened as things began to fall into place. It wasn't crazy talk. It wasn't hallucinations.

My mother's last words.

The warning from Allegra.

I sniffled and rubbed my nose.

The lights flickered.

I rubbed my nose again, and the lights flickered again.

I drilled my eyes into Bessie, and she nodded.

"No." I set Cooper on the ground and jumped from my seat,

running my hand through my hair and then dragging it down my chin. "No." I laughed because really, what else could I do? It was ludicrous, impossible. Ridiculous. It was fiction. Esmerelda's world. Not mine.

Or was it?

Bessie stood next to me, wrapped her arm around my shaking shoulders, and pointed to a bookshelf nearby. "See that pile of books?"

I nodded.

"Watch."

I shivered.

"It'll be fine, sweetie. I promise." She flicked her hand in the air, and the books fell to the ground.

My entire body stiffened and then shook violently.

She flicked her hand again and they repositioned themselves back on top of the shelf.

My eyes stayed the size of saucers. I gulped down a mouth full of air and choked. I couldn't stop coughing.

"Oh, dear. I shouldn't have done it that way." She held onto my arm and guided me the few steps back to the table. "Here, sit. I'll get you some water."

I waved her off as my coughing slowed. "No, it's okay. I'm... I'm good." I took a deep breath and let it out slowly. "What's wrong with me?"

"Nothing is wrong with you honey, in fact, everything is right with you now. This is a gift, a gift to be treasured."

My thoughts tangled into a jumbled knot, and hard as I tried to focus, to allow myself to speak, all I could do was stutter. "I... I...am I..."

She scooted closer to me. "How about we start at the beginning?"

I couldn't even begin to imagine where that was. I white knuckled the seat of the chair, knowing that my life had completely changed forever and wondering if I'd ever feel right again.

"What made you decide to write about witches?"

I furrowed my brow. I'd never actually thought about the reason behind my character. She just sort of evolved of her own accord. When I explained that to Bessie, she disagreed.

"We're led to things that matter, things in our lives which shape us, Abby, whether it's consciously or unconsciously. You didn't choose to write about witches, and warlocks, and shapeshifters. They chose you because of who you are."

"I think you mean what I am."

"Everyone is unique. Each of us have something special only to us, be it Merlock's cranky personality, or say, Peter's fun-loving sense of humor. But those special things don't define us, they aren't what we are, they just help shape and define *who* we are."

"Okay then, who am I?"

"You're Abigail Odell."

I wanted her to say it. I thought it, and I felt strongly that what I thought was the thing she dodged, but I needed to hear it out loud, as if that would make it true. Make it possible. "You know what I mean."

She grabbed my hand and squeezed tight. "Abigail Odell, you're a witch."

CHAPTER 3

*E*xactly how someone went about coming to terms with the sentence, *you're a witch*, was lost on me. Not that people ever really heard that kind of thing, or that that kind of thing actually existed in the real world. It couldn't.

Witches lived inside the minds of little girls, little girls who've read *Snow White*, watched *The Wizard of Oz*. Witches took busy, exhausted moms from their reality and transported them to another world. Witches didn't sit inside bookstores, chat, and drink coffee, but yes, they did. Regardless of how much I wanted to deny it, to not believe it, to ignore it, it was true, and I knew it down deep in my bones.

I stared at her in disbelief, no, more like shock, listening to her as she shared the details of the Odell family. I sat in anxious anticipation, biting my nail and tapping my foot as she explained how my mother did a binding spell on my powers, fully expecting at some point to explain everything to me and offer me the choice in unbinding them or staying human-like forever, something she could arrange, Bessie said. She said my mother never intended to die without that explanation, but since she had, the spell was lifted, and my powers came out like a wrestler in the final round of a match.

I blinked.

"You have a question."

"I have a lot of questions."

She leaned back in her seat and waved her hand in the air. The coffee pot floated over and she topped off our cups while my mouth gaped and my blood pressure rose. "I really wish your mother would have been here for this. She was always so much better at explaining things."

My mother? Explaining things? I had to laugh at that. My mother was the fun loving, fly by the seat of her pants parent. Bessie had always been the clear-headed, logical parental figure in my life.

A light flashed outside, and the door burst opened. A gust of fierce wind blew in, lifting books and magazines from their spots and swirling them into an intense funnel in the middle of the store.

My hair whipped across my face making it almost impossible for me to see. "What's going on?" I screamed. A book whipped past me, barely missing my head. I covered my face with my hands. "This is crazy!"

The funnel slowly took the form of a man. I stood with my feet frozen to the ground, my heart racing, and my mind running a close second behind it as the books and magazines fell to the ground around Merlock Dupe. Every part of my body locked in place. I couldn't even blink.

Bessie set her chair upright and tucked it under the table. "Merlock Dupe, did your momma not teach you any manners?"

He tucked his chin into his neck and spoke to Bessie like a kindergartener who'd just been caught doing something wrong in class. "I don't like the coffee at the Corner Café."

I watched in awe as Bessie rolled her eyes and threw her arms up in the air. "You," she said, pointing at the man, "are a pain in my behind. Now clean this up, and I'll give you a refill, but just one. I'm having a talk with Abby here."

He nodded, and as he raised his arms, a flash of light exploded in the room, blinding me for a straight five seconds. I had to close my eyes for fear they'd burn from the brightness. When I opened them, everything was back in its original spot. I rubbed my eyes to make sure I wasn't imagining it, and I wasn't.

"May I have my refill now?"

Bessie exhaled. "Excuse me," she said, and scurried around the counter to the coffee pot.

I couldn't take my eyes off Merlock. The grouchy, Eeyore-like old man I'd known nearly all my life had...had gone all Father Nature inside the small store.

Bessie refilled his cup. "I gave you a special recipe. Try not to pitch another fit like that, okay? You know what it does to you."

Merlock bowed his head again and nodded. "I know. I know." He smiled at me, said, "Welcome to the family, Abby," and then turned around and left.

I picked up my chair, set it upright, fell into it and then jumped right back out. "Where's Mr. Charming?" I shifted back and forth, searching the room. "And Cooper!" I rushed over to the chair in the front window display and found Cooper snoozing under it. I scooped him up and cradled him in my arms, kissing his nose and head repeatedly. Mr. Charming flew over from the back of the store and perched on Bessie's shoulder.

Bessie rubbed the parrot's feet. "He's used to Merlock's episodes. He knows to hide or he'll get whipped up in the mess, like that cow in the *Wizard of Oz* movie." She held out her other arm and he jumped to it. "Don't you, good boy?"

"Good boy. I'm a good boy."

I dragged myself back to my chair, placed Cooper on the table, and buried my head in my hands. "Unbelievable," I muttered. "Un-freaking-believable." I'd stepped right into

Esmerelda's world where magic lived, no thrived, and I couldn't wrap my mind around any of it.

Bessie patted me on the back. "You've got a lot to learn, but you'll figure it out. In the meantime, we need to talk about Allegra."

My head shot up. "You know Allegra?"

She nodded slowly, giving me a small, guilty look in the process. "Everyone knows Allegra, or knew her back in the day."

"But me. You forgot that. Everyone but me knows Allegra. I didn't even know she existed."

She sighed. "Ah, yes. The black sheep of the family rarely ever get recognition." She cleared her throat. "Your mother warned me about this. She feared they would return. Now we just have to find the other one and take care of him."

They? Other one? Him? What in the devil was she talking about?

She raised her eyebrows and shook her head once. "Addie had wicked intuition." She locked her eyes with mine and winked. "No pun intended of course, and she took precautions in case this happened, but with your powers so new to you, this could be complicated."

I opened my mouth to say something, but nothing came out. I couldn't even think words let alone say them.

"I know this is a lot to take in, and like I said, your mother would have preferred telling you herself, but we can't control fate." She tapped her finger on the table. "There are many things we can control, but that's a conversation for another time."

I'd yet to close my mouth or get a word out of it.

"Yes, okay. Allegra." She tapped her fingers on the table again. "Where do I start?"

"How about the beginning? Like, with how it's possible for witches to be real? That would be a great place, don't you think?" Cooper crawled onto my chest and nuzzled his head into my neck.

"Yes, we'll get there, but we've got to handle this first."

"Okay." The word shook as I said it.

"Allegra and Samuel Odell were banned from the family, and subsequently Holiday Hills, before you were born." She rubbed her chin and glanced up at the ceiling. "It was just a few months after your parents announced they were expecting. The entire town was thrilled about you." Her eyes unfocused as she gazed up again, clearly in the midst of a happy memory. "A powerful warlock and an even more powerful witch were bound to create a magical child with incredible strength. Everyone wanted to see that."

Cooper snored in my ear like Bessie and I were just hanging out, casually talking about something unimportant and not the fact that my family heritage included something I'd always considered make believe.

"Well, not everyone. Allegra and Samuel, they were jealous of your mother. Always had been, too. She was your grandparents favorite, and not because of her powers. You know your mom, everyone loved her. And that affection, well, it wasn't the same for Allegra and Samuel." She made a snickering sound. "Samuel, he was as exciting as a hole in the wall. And Allegra, well, she was a witch, just swap the w for a b, you know what I mean?"

I rushed her to her point. "What does this all have to do with me?"

She exhaled. "Once you were born, they knew they would be irrelevant, useless even, and they'd lose their spots in the family line." She pressed her lips together. "The family line. We'll have to talk about that another time. I'll keep to the basics for now."

From the sound of things, Bessie and I would spend the rest of my life talking.

"And the only way to maintain their status—unpopular as it may have been—was to, you know." She tilted her head.

"Get rid of me?"

She nodded.

I swallowed hard. "So, you think Allegra was here to kill me?"

"I'm not there yet. Let me finish."

She sipped her coffee. I hadn't even seen her pour herself another cup, but I didn't question it. I had far too many questions rolling around in my brain. They bounced off the sides of my head, intensifying my already throbbing headache.

"Two months before you were born, Allegra, Samuel, and three shapeshifters attacked your mother and father in the middle of the night."

She'd all but lost me at shapeshifters, and she must have realized that because she patted my leg. "I know this is a lot, but you'll get it, I promise."

I nodded, fighting back the tears pooling in my eyes, though I knew I'd never *get it*.

"Your mother was ready. That intuition didn't always predict the future, and magic doesn't tell us everything, but it did warn her, and she knew. She and your father were prepared to fight, but three shapeshifters, a witch, and a warlock? That was practically impossible. They fought hard, they really did. And your father, Abby, your father was a hero. He sacrificed himself to save you and your mother."

I let the tears out then, let them fall down my face. My mother told me stories of my father, of their love, promised me he'd loved me with every bit of his soul, swore he would do anything for me, and she wasn't exaggerating. He had. He died so I could live.

"Your mother was a powerful witch, one of the most powerful ones I've ever met, but pregnancy plays tricks on powers, and regardless, five against two was a losing battle from the start. She weakened, and in a moment of brutal battle, your father stepped in front of her, protecting the two of you from the deadly attack of a shapeshifter. Your mother was able to project herself away. To her dying day she couldn't forgive herself for not projecting your father, but everyone told her it was fate, and like I said, we can't control everything. It was your father's time."

I wrapped my arms around Cooper, and he climbed higher on my chest.

"When her father found out, he stripped them of their powers and banished them from the family."

"Where did they go?"

She shrugged. "We weren't allowed to know. He put a hiding spell on them, meaning we were hidden from them, and they were hidden from us. Your mother felt awful. She was devastated and afraid. She left shortly after you were born, but in time, when she felt safe, she returned."

"But if there was a hiding spell, how did Allegra find us?"

"Like I said, pregnancy is tricky. Your grandfather thought he'd cast the hiding spell on you, too, but," she shrugged. "I guess it didn't work. Your mother worried about that, but I don't think she planned for things to happen this soon. She didn't expect she'd die without you knowing."

I didn't need to be a genius to figure things out. "Now my uncle is after me, but why? What's it matter now?"

"Your uncle knows if he kills you, he can have your power."

Great. I've got a black sheep warlock with years of pent up anger gunning for me. "Why now? Why not do this years ago?"

"Only active powers can be stolen."

"So why not kill my mother? That would have released the spell—" My eyes widened, and my heart pounded so hard I thought it would burst through my chest. "Do you think he…"

She grabbed my hands and squeezed them tight. "I can't be sure, and I don't think we'll ever know the truth."

She was wrong. I knew. It burned a hole deep inside the pit of my soul. Samuel Odell murdered my mother, and he was coming for me.

* * *

Bessie and I spent four more hours going over the minute

details of my family history. We tacked on another hour for a detailed explanation of Holiday Hills, a town designed for magicals of all kinds by magicals determined to live together in harmony. That explained our low crime rate, and the fact that everyone appeared to be besties with everyone else, but it didn't explain how they–or we—lived among humans without their knowledge. And there were humans in Holiday Hills. My best friend included.

I toyed with the idea of sharing the secret with Stella, but Bessie cautioned me against it. Humans don't understand, she said, and no matter how close I felt to Stella, believing the unbelievable was asking the impossible.

Stella wanted a pizza and Hallmark movie night, claiming she needed some down time, but she couldn't fool me. She worried about me sitting alone at night wallowing in my grief.

"I've got to go to my mom's place tonight. I need to take care of some things and at least get started cleaning it out." I pressed my lips together wondering if that was actually possible. I did need to do all of that, but my reason for going had more to do with discovering something, anything, to make sense of my new, twisted reality.

"You sure? It's not like you're on a timeline or anything. How about I come help?"

"Stel, really, I'm fine. I'm sure I'll want your help another time, but I kind of just want to be there alone, you know?"

"I understand. Call me if you need me?"

"Always." I disconnected the call as I pulled into my mother's driveway.

When Zach and I divorced, Mom wanted me to move back in with her, but I couldn't bring myself to run home to momma. The house wasn't large by any means, but it was definitely big enough for two, and she'd left my room empty, as if it was just waiting for my things to fill it again. But as much as I loved that old A-frame cottage, I needed to be on my own.

Mr. Charming climbed up my arm and planted himself on my shoulder as I shut the car door. Temperatures in the north Georgia mountains often dropped to freezing during the long winter nights, and that night it was close. Mr. Charming shivered on my arm, and Cooper, usually a laid back and lazy cat that wouldn't run if his life depended on it, charged to the front door. I took his loud meowing as a call to hurry up.

I unlocked the door and Cooper rushed in. Mr. Charming dug his claws into my shoulder and repeated what my mother said to him every time she returned home. "Hello, sweetie pie. I'm home. I'm home."

My heart sank. The poor bird missed our mom as much as me. I leaned my head into his green body. "I miss her too, buddy."

He flew off my shoulder and perched onto his parrot tree in the small family room. "Hello, sweetie pie. I'm home. I'm home."

I locked the door behind me, twisting and re-twisting the three bolts to make sure they were secure.

Bessie explained that since I knew I was a—I wasn't quite able to say the actual word, even to myself—things would be different, that they'd look and feel strange at first, but that I'd eventually adjust. She also said magic would show itself slowly. Baby steps for the baby, I assumed. My mother's house didn't look any different, but I felt as if something had changed. The stale air of a house left stagnant for days maybe, the emptiness of breath, or maybe the lack of magic. I wasn't sure, but I couldn't decide if I should attribute the change in the air to magic or to the fact that I hadn't been there since she'd passed. When the lights on her Christmas tree flashed on and her record player spun a Frank Sinatra Christmas song, I figured it was something I'd done.

Mr. Charming chirped as he looped throughout the first floor of his home. "Where's my baby? Where's my baby?"

A tear formed in my eye, but I wiped it away. Bessie said my mother kept a box she'd planned to give to me when she told me the truth. She kept it locked in a small safe built into the wall in the family room, hidden behind a large painting of my grandparents. I stared at the painting, suddenly seeing the grandparents I'd never met with a new eye. Maybe even a magical eye.

They didn't seem any different than the last time I'd admired the painting. My grandmother, a round, chunky woman with silver hair cut short to frame her face. Her pale skin wrinkled, but not enough to show her actual age. My grandfather, a taller, thinner man with a military style haircut, high and tight my mother called it. His blue eyes magnified in his large glasses. I'd always loved how they'd both worn cream colored clothing and wondered if they'd matched on purpose.

I pushed the chair aside, and Cooper jumped up onto it, rested his squatty body on the top, as he stared intently at my grandparents.

I patted him on the head. "Looks like life's going to get interesting, little guy."

He purred.

I removed the painting, gently set it on the floor and leaned it against the wall. Bessie didn't know the combination. She'd assured me I would. I examined the small lock, thinking up numbers to try. My birthday? I twisted the lock to the right, then back to the left and landed on the line for the eight, then I twisted it once to the left until I landed on the line for the eleven, and then around completely and then back to the line for the sixteen.

The lock popped open. I had to laugh at how well my mother knew me. I had my first school locker in sixth grade, and I was so excited to finally be with the big kids in middle school, the first thing I wanted to do was get my combination lock for my locker. I had that lock all through school, including college for the gym, though I'd barely used it then, and continued to use it on those rare days Stella dragged me kicking and screaming like a toddler to her gym.

I took a deep breath and said, "Here we go," to Cooper as I opened the safe door.

Only two things were in the small safe: a thick white candle, partially used, and an old, tattered and torn leather-bound book. I took them out and got comfortable on the couch knowing I had a long night ahead of me. Cooper jumped from the chair to the couch and curled up next to my side. Mr. Charming flew into the room and planted himself on the back of the couch. I opened the book to a handwritten note just beneath the cover.

Abby, if you're reading this, I'm sorry I'm not there for you. This book belonged to our ancestors, and it's filled with spells to help you navigate through life, and to help you learn how to use your powers effectively. Treat this book with love, but use it with caution because it's very, very powerful. And Abby, there are two things you must never, ever forget.

You cannot use your powers for personal gain. Second, no human must ever know you're a magical. No matter how close you are, no matter how much that person loves you, or you love them, they must never know. There are many reasons for this, but the only one that matters is this: their knowing puts them in great danger.

My love, you're now in an amazing, beautiful world, and I so wish I could be there to share it with you. Do good things, and remember, I'm always with you. Love, Mom.

I wiped the tears from my eyes and rubbed my nose. The book closed. I groaned. "Seriously, that's going to be a royal pain in the butt."

Cooper lifted his head but set it back down again without so much as a groan.

"Gee, thanks for the support." I opened the book again and gently flipped through the crisp, old pages. The paper was so old, its color passed yellow and bordered on a light brown. Pieces were taped together by tape that lost its stickiness years ago. I carefully set the book down on the coffee table and stepped over to my mother's desk to retrieve a roll of tape just in case something came apart. *Treat this book with love.*

Once comfy on the couch again, I began reading. The book, a virtual how-to for witches, included spells for simple things like easing someone's pain to creating a thunderstorm. I wondered how many of the spells my mother used on me over the years. Had magic helped me pass my AP Chemistry class senior year in high school? Through my divorce?

The book pages turned themselves, landing on a page with a hand drawn cat. "Woah, Cooper, this cat looks almost exactly like you."

Cooper lifted his head, placed it on the edge of the book, and then went right back to sleep. I read the words on the page, a spell, it said, to arouse my familiar. A familiar? I stared at Cooper. Esmerelda had a familiar, of course, but like other magical things, I considered them folklore.

The spell called for a lit candle, so I hoisted the heavy book back to the table and dug through the desk for a match book or lighter. I kept the book on the table and lit the candle, then said the spell out loud. *Those that came before me, I call upon thee, allow the soul of my familiar to appear to me. Let them be here, in my time of need, and keep them safe while protecting me.*

Make us one, my familiar and I, and keep us safe under your loving eye.

I expected lights to flash, the music to blast loudly, or thunder to crack—something, but nope. Nothing happened. The candle flame flickered a little as Cooper stood and stretched, but that was about it.

Mr. Charming flew off the back of the couch and to his cage, where he munched on a few seeds. Obviously, he was as unimpressed as I was.

"Well, that was useless."

Cooper stretched his front leg to the coffee table and hopped onto it, taking a seat next to the book. "It's about time."

My eyes popped, and my mouth gaped open, though I couldn't form words. I tilted my head and stared at my cat.

"Yeah, yeah, I know. I'm talking. I get it. You're freaking out." He licked his paw. When he finished, he shook his little body and meowed. "You'll get used to it."

My cat spoke. Words. From his mouth. Words. "I, uh…" I tilted my head again.

"That dog you had used to do that all the time. I liked to talk human to him and watch him do that head tilt thing." He licked his other paw. "Dog was a pain sometimes, shoving his nose into my face and dragging his nasty tongue up my mouth and nose." His body shivered. "Breath smelled like dirt."

I managed to get one word out. "Dog?"

"Yeah, dog. You know, the one that Zach loser had. You called him Brutus, but yeah, that wasn't his name. His real name was Harvey, but he got used to Brutus. And don't get me started on that Zach. The stories I could tell." He waited for me to say something, but I just sat there, my mouth gaping open like a child who'd been busted doing something they weren't supposed to. "Listen Abby, it's going to be okay. You'll get used to this, I promise."

I shook my head, working desperately to clear the crazy out of my brain. I closed my eyes, took a deep breath, and then opened them slowly.

Cooper stared at me. "Still here. Still talking."

"Deep breaths, Abby." I tried hard not to hyperventilate. "Deep breaths."

My talking cat kept his eyes focused on me. I glanced at Mr. Charming snacking on seeds. "Can…is…"

"Nope. Not to you anyway. He was Addie's familiar. He's sticking around until," he paused. "Until we fix things. Then he'll either find another witch, or he'll go to Addie, or not. Never can tell what that bird will do."

My eyes widened even further. "You mean he could die?"

Cooper shook his head. "Oh, no. Sorry, didn't mean to freak you out like that. I mean he'll go to her. You know, his soul. Familiars tend to stick to their witches, or their powers anyway, but some of us like to find new ones. We like to stick around."

I shook my head again, trying to wrap it around the idea that I was having a conversation with my cat, and that my cat was actually talking back.

He jumped back to the couch and stood on the arm closest to me. "Okay, here's the thing. I know you're in shock, and I get that. I mean, your cat's talking to you, but come on, you write this stuff, what'd you think, someone made it up?"

I nodded.

"Well, you know they didn't, and we've got a lot to do, so you need to suck it up, buttercup."

I blinked.

"I'll give you a minute to grasp the complexity of a talking cat and then we'll get to work, okay?" He lifted his back leg and licked himself.

That took on a whole new, disgusting meaning for me.

When he stopped, he made eye contact again and said, "You good now?"

I blinked again. "I'm not sure that's even possible."

"I can't wait for you to come to terms with this. We've got to deal with Samuel, and now."

The pages of the book flipped and stopped about a quarter of the way through.

"I love that thing," Cooper said.

I read the page to myself, and Cooper meowed. "You do know cats can't read, right?"

I rolled my eyes. "I didn't know they could talk but look at you."

His chillaxed attitude disappeared. "Just tell me what the book says."

I chewed on my fingernail as I read the page to myself first.

"It's a discovery spell." I pressed my lips together and thought about that. "What am I supposed to discover?"

Cooper got comfy on the table. "You're a newbie. There's a lot left to discover."

"Well, yeah, obviously, but you'd think this thing would be a little clearer with the details."

"It's a book of spells, not a textbook."

I groaned. "I'm not really comfortable with casting spells that don't make sense to me. I don't want to get in over my head." As if I wasn't already drowning in the sea of the unknown and unbelievable.

"Abby, you've got a warlock after you. One that most likely killed two of his sisters to get your powers. You don't have time to get comfortable."

I closed the book. "Maybe not, but I have to do things my way, on my terms."

"Why?"

Because I'm stubborn and don't like taking orders from a book didn't sound like the right answer, so instead I said, "Because I don't understand any of this, and I...I need time to let it all soak in, you know? What if I do something wrong and I, I don't know, I blow up the town, or hurt someone I love?"

"That book is designed to protect and help you. If you get in over your head, it'll be because you didn't listen to it, not because you did what it asked."

"Says a cat that can't read."

"I've been around the block a time or two."

"Exactly, and from what I know, you're my familiar, so if anything happens to me, you'll protect me, right? I don't need to do anything in that book. I've got you."

He rolled onto his back and faced the opposite direction. "See that bird over there?"

I groaned again. "Yes."

"He was brought here to protect your mother."

My shoulders sank. He had a point, and it was a good one.

"I am here to protect you, but I can only do so much."

I stared at the book, ready to open it and search the pages for the discovery spell, but I didn't have to. It flipped open again to that exact page.

"See? You can't run from the book."

I narrowed my eyes at my previously favorite pet.

"Read it out loud."

I inhaled, counted to five, and then exhaled. "Others before me, hear my plea. Show me the evil coming after me." I stopped. "What? No. I'm not reading this. It wants me to bring Samuel to me."

"No, Abby. It wants you to see Samuel so you can identify him when he's near. You can't fight a warlock if you don't know where he is."

"Nope. I'm not doing it." I closed the book again. "I'm not prepared to deal with this Samuel just yet. Every time I touch my ear or my nose, stuff happens. Don't you think I should get a handle on that before I try to fight off someone with a heck of a lot more experience than me?"

He nodded. "His powers were bound, remember?"

"Doesn't mean he hasn't picked some up along the way."

My mother.

"Tell you what, better safe than sorry, right? How about we practice just in case."

"Practice what?"

"The nose thing. You know, give it a whirl, see how it works."

"But my mother said I can't use my powers for personal gain."

"Personal gain is to, I don't know, say conjure up a can of tuna when you're hungry."

"I don't eat tuna."

"No, not you. Me. If I were to conjure up a can of tuna, it would be personal gain for me. But you? You'd be doing it for your cat." He scooted to the edge of the table. "Come to think of it, that's a great place to start practicing. Go on, give it a shot."

"What am I supposed to do, think about tuna and touch my nose?"

"Worth a try, right?"

"Tuna, tuna, tuna," I said, repeating it as I rubbed beneath my nose.

Cans of tuna appeared on the table next to Cooper.

His tail whipped back and forth. "Yeah, baby. That's what I'm talking about."

I rolled my eyes, but inside, my excitement did somersaults in my stomach.

"Can you get a can opener? I don't want them all, just one for now. Got to keep my strength up to stave off your uncle, you know."

I thought about a can opener and tapped the tip of my nose.

Boom, a can opener landed behind my cat.

"I'm digging this now," he said.

"Except the can isn't open."

He stepped over the can opener and used a paw to shove it toward the edge of the table. "I could use some help." He propped up on his hind legs and held his front paws up. "No opposable thumbs."

I opened the can, and Cooper made his typical moaning sounds as he ate, but he added words to it. "Yum, wow. I love me some tuna. Moan, moan. This is so good."

I rolled my eyes.

When he finished, he licked his mouth and pushed the can to the side. "Okay, I'm ready to get serious now."

"Yay."

He flipped around and examined the small room. "How about you get that tchotchke over there on the shelf? The one with the angel's what's it called over its head."

"Halo?"

He nodded.

I stood and walked toward the small angel.

"No. Not like that." He sighed. "Do your nose thing."

I tapped my nose and thought about the tchotchke. It floated over to me. I smiled. I couldn't help myself.

"Good, good. Yeah, you're getting the hang of it."

"So, I'm channeling my inner Prue Halliwell. What good does that do me?"

"Who's Prue Halliwell?"

"She's a character on a—" I waved it off. "Never mind. I just don't see how moving things with my mind is going to help me with Samuel."

"Ah, the newbie. So uneducated and so naïve."

I narrowed my eyes at my cat as I sat back on the couch. "I liked you better when you didn't talk."

He ignored that. "You're special. You know that. You're not just able to move things with your mind. Look at the tuna. You conjured it. By yourself."

"And?"

"You don't get it, do you?"

I shook my head.

"You can control things with your mind. That's basically a limitless power. You want to freeze someone like Piper Halliwell—"

"Hey, I thought—"

"I paid attention while you watched *Charmed*. Mostly because I wanted to see how close they got to reality, and it was entertaining. Totally fiction, but entertaining."

"So, there aren't evil beings out to get me?"

"Evil is alive and well in both the human and magical worlds, but it's not like the show."

"I guess that's good to know." I pursed my lips. "But Bessie can move things with her mind, too."

"Big difference there."

"I'm missing that."

"She can move things, can command them to her. If Bessie wanted a cup of coffee, but there wasn't coffee in the store, she couldn't get it. If you want a can of tuna, which you never buy for me because you don't love me as much as you say, all you have to do is think about it, and wa-la, it's here." He swiped his tongue across his mouth. "Command verses conjure. Big difference.

"Abby, Samuel doesn't have his powers. Your grandfather made sure of that. He was able to cast a spell strong enough to remove your aunt and uncle's powers permanently. But Samuel isn't dumb. He knows there are ways to get powers from other witches and warlocks."

"How?"

"That's the one part of *Charmed* that was kind of true."

I didn't like the way that sounded. "Please explain."

"When a witch dies, if another witch or warlock is there, they can take their powers as the soul releases itself from the body, if they catch it in time."

"Even a warlock that doesn't have any powers?"

He nodded. "It's not easy, but like I said, Samuel's not dumb." He stared at me. "This gets complicated. You might want to take notes."

I rolled my eyes. "Just tell me."

"Okay, most of the time, it goes like this. Not always, but I have a feeling it's the case with your mom. You see, when a witch dies, like I said before, their familiar usually goes with them. Sometimes they stick around for unfinished business, and sometimes—"

"You already told me this. They attach themselves to another magical."

"Yeah, but I didn't tell you why. Baby steps, right?"

I folded my arms across my chest. "Go on."

"A familiar will only attach itself to another magical if their first one's powers transferred to the magical. They go with the power to protect it and return it to whom it belongs. And that doesn't always happen. The familiar could stay to protect someone else or something." He glanced at my mother's parrot. "Seeing as the bird's still here…"

"You don't think Samuel got my mother's powers, do you?"

"Ah newbie, you've got so much to learn."

"Then give me the *Reader's Digest* version."

"The Odell family is a powerful family, and your mother's powers were strong. She could have cast some kind of spell to stop him from getting them. It wouldn't be easy, given her weakened state and all, but I'd say it's definitely possible."

"I'm confused."

He studied his front paw, licked it, and then said, "Won't be the first time."

"If Samuel doesn't have any powers, how exactly did he murder my mom? She'd been sick for weeks. The doctor said her illness was too much for her heart, and it simply stopped while she slept. Samuel couldn't make her heart just stop."

"You're right. That's the part I'm stuck on."

"What if Samuel isn't here? What if the spell my grandfather cast wasn't broken, and we're still hidden from him? What if this is something else entirely?"

"Then how do you explain Allegra?"

He had a point. If my grandfather's spell wasn't broken, then Allegra couldn't have found us. Adding the fact that Allegra was dead, none of it made any sense. I pushed a loose strand of hair from my face. "Allegra was shot. Would a warlock shoot someone?"

"He would if he couldn't use magic to kill them."

"Okay, so let me see if I've got this straight." I tilted my head and thought about it all for a moment, letting everything sink in as far as my shocked mind would let it. "Samuel and Allegra had their powers bound and they were banned from the family. My mother bound my powers to keep me safe because she feared they would find me, and I don't know, what? Kill me so they could get my powers?"

"I'm guessing that's what she feared."

I tugged my lower lip between the side of my front teeth. "And even though Mom died in her sleep, it's possible Samuel—"

"It's starting to make a little sense now, isn't it?"

"But Allegra? Why kill her? And why did she leave me that note? Why did she talk to me at Mom's life celebration? If she wanted my powers, why not just kill me and take them?"

"That's another part that stumps me."

I glared at him.

"Hey, don't look at me that way. I'm not a psychic. I'm a cat with a little something extra."

"Maybe I could conjure Allegra's spirit and find out what happened? Or even my mom's spirit!"

"Oh boy. I wouldn't go there. Messing with the dead and that portal, it's tricky for an experienced witch, but for a newbie like you? You could really mess things up."

"Mess things up how?"

"You've got to be careful with the in-between. Once you open that portal, you can't be sure what steps through it. You're not ready for that. Besides, you don't just conjure a spirit and ask it to tell you what you want to know. It doesn't work that way."

"Why not?"

"Because it doesn't. You're only given what you need to know when you need to know it. I'm sure I'll have to say this a bunch of times to let it sink in, but it's true. The universe has rules, and a lot of them are stiffer for magicals than humans."

I sighed. "So, what you're saying is I have to figure this out on my own."

"You want my opinion?"

"Yeah, the opinion of my cat has always been important to me." My tone bled sarcasm.

"Don't worry about Allegra. She's gone. Worry about Samuel. You find him, you get your answers, then you get rid of him. Easy peasy."

"What do you mean get rid of him?"

"You know, send him off with a bang. Kick him out the door. Make him into dog food, that kind of thing."

"You want me to kill my uncle?"

"You gotta do what you gotta do to survive, Abby."

I jumped from the couch and paced the room. "I am not killing my uncle. I'm…I'm…I'm not a murderer."

Cooper climbed off the table, walked over to the shelf where the angel had been, and hopped onto its top. "That's your call, but all I'm saying is that's probably a good idea."

"You're a cat. You're designed to hunt and kill your prey. It's innate in your DNA."

"There is that."

"There's always another side. Another way to deal with a situation, or something hidden in the story that changes things. That's how I write my books. Who's to say that's not happening here?"

"Like I said, I don't read."

I hurried to my mother's desk and grabbed a pad of paper from the top drawer. I plucked a pencil from the cup and went back to the couch. I jotted down a few thoughts, tapped the pencil tip to my lips, and jotted down a few more.

Cooper hopped onto the table and sat directly on top of the pad of paper. "You gonna share any of that scribbling with me?"

"Everyone loved my mom, right?"

"I got that impression."

"And Mr. Charming's still here, so that means he's got some sort of unfinished business, right?"

"Like sticking to her magic so he can return it to her? Yeah."

"And Allegra came to my mother's life celebration, then she went to the family tomb, and someone killed her there."

"You're not telling me anything I don't already know."

"Maybe she wasn't after my powers. Maybe she was here to protect me, or to warn me, and maybe it's not about Samuel."

He curled himself into a ball on the paper. "You lost me."

"What if it's someone else? What if someone else wants my powers?" I pulled the pad out from under him. "Practically everyone in town is a magical, and they'd know I am, too. They'd also probably realize that when my mom died, her binding spell would end, and my powers would come to life."

"You think someone in town is trying to kill you?"

"I think I just added thousands of people to my suspect list." I stared at the book of spells, and then at my cat, then at the book again. "Show me a spell that lets me see other's true intentions."

The book stayed shut.

"Remember what I said a few minutes ago?"

"I'm only given what I need to know when I need to know it."

"That's my girl."

Frustration and defeat pumped through my veins. Someone was out to get me, and I had amazing powers and a magical book to stop it, but I felt useless. I reached for Cooper and then jerked my arms back. I wanted to pick him up and cuddle him close to me like I used to, but that just seemed awkward and uncomfortable.

"It's okay. I won't bite. Not you anyway."

"It's weird."

"You'll get used to it. I promise I'll keep my mouth shut most of the time. Just keep the cans of tuna coming, and we'll be good."

I released a long, warm breath, feeling like my whole body needed to discharge a mountains worth of anxiety. "This is a lot to take in."

"I bet it is, but you're smart. You'll get the hang of it."

"So, what do I do next?"

"If you think someone in town wants your powers, then you've got to figure that out."

"So, you believe me?"

"I'm not here to believe or not believe. I'm here to support. But I will say this. Witches have good intuition. You follow that and you'll figure it out."

"What happens if I do? Am I supposed to, you know, eliminate the person?"

"It's not a person who's coming after you, Abby."

"Still."

"How about we worry about that if and when we need to?"

"Deal."

He hopped onto my lap, snuggled up into a little ball, and yawned. "Time to nap. I'm behind on my eighteen hours of sleep."

CHAPTER 4

*S*tella sat at my table and set up her laptop. She lifted the lid and typed in her log in. "So, how'd it go last night?"

Oh, let's see. I cast a spell from my mom's spell book, and my cat and I spent most of the night talking about who might possibly be trying to kill me to gain my witch powers. "Fine."

She tilted her head. "Fine? That's all you're going to say?"

I broke off a piece of my chocolate chip cookie and popped it into my mouth. "I didn't go through anything. I just kind of hung out."

She held my hand. "It's hard, I know. I'm here to help, okay?"

I pulled my hand away. "I know. I just have to get this book done, and then I can deal with everything else." I needed to distance myself from Stella. What if whomever, or whatever, gunning for me hurt her? I couldn't let that happen.

"If there isn't a problem…"

"Trust me, I'm not avoiding the issue. I promise."

"I know, and in this case, I'd understand. You don't have to go through your mom's things right away. They're not going anywhere."

"I know."

Merlock and Peter walked in, arguing about something I knew meant nothing in the grand scheme of things.

"That ain't the way it works, old man, Peter said. He guided himself into his regular chair. "You either pay what you owe, or you suffer the consequences."

I kept one ear locked on the men as Stella rambled on about my book.

Bessie handed Merlock his coffee, and he sat. "Your consequences don't worry me. What're you going to do, beat me up?"

Peter coughed as Merlock disappeared into a cloud of dust. The dust swirled into a mini funnel cloud. I stared at Stella, who'd begun typing something into her computer, oblivious to what happened a few feet away from her.

A gnarly haired gray wolf growled as the dust settled.

Bessie shook her finger at the wolf. "Now Merlock, you know I don't like you shifting at my store. It scares some of the customers."

My eyes widened and my mouth gaped open. I looked at Stella and then back at Merlock, pointing at the hairy wolf. "He's...he's..."

Stella flipped around and shrugged. "They're arguing like they always do. Probably about football."

She didn't see it. She didn't see Merlock the wolf, only Merlock the man. I wondered how many times he'd done that before? How many times he'd done it and I didn't see.

The bell on the door chimed and chief of police, Gabe Ryder walked in. He removed his hat and smiled at Bessie, Peter, and wolf Merlock. I couldn't say for sure but given his expression—lips curved upward instead of snarled—Gabe saw the man version of Merlock, too.

Which meant Gabe wasn't a magical.

Bessie gave him a cup of coffee, and he stepped over to my table. He tipped his head once. "Ladies."

"Good morning, Chief," Stella said, all smiles while she kicked my leg under the table.

I shot her a stern look. "Chief Ryder."

"Ms. Odell, if you have some time today, I'm going to need you to come down to the station to answer a few questions."

Wolf Merlock disappeared into a cloud of dust, and human Merlock reappeared. I tried to not let him distract me, shaking my head and directing my eyes back to the police chief. "I'm sorry, what did you say?"

Stella kicked me under the table again.

"Ow."

"I'd like you to come to the station this morning. I've got some questions for you."

"Questions, about what?"

"How about we discuss it at the station, say thirty minutes?"

I furrowed my brow. "Uh, okay, sure."

He tipped his head again, sipped his coffee, and left the store.

"Oh, look at that." Stella clapped her hands and made a little cheering sound. "Looks like you've got yourself a morning rendezvous with your secret crush."

The dead weight in my stomach didn't agree. "I'm pretty sure he's not asking me for a social visit."

I made eye contact with Bessie and her furrowed brow confirmed she thought the same thing.

Stella's smile faded. "Then why?" She leaned back in her chair and sipped her drink. "Did you park in a no parking zone or something? Maybe he wants to reprimand you in private."

I played it off as nothing serious. "I'm sure it's something like that."

* * *

.   .   .

I f you excluded the jail, the Holiday Hills Police Department wasn't much bigger than The Enchanted. A small waiting area with four metal chairs lining the side walls, national and state flags hanging on one wall, and plaques with photos of football and baseball teams sponsored by the department on the other. I waited in a chair there, watching the other side of the glass partition for signs of life. I'd rung the bell, and just as I stood to do so again, Chief Ryder walked through the door from behind the glass.

He escorted me into his office and directed me to a hard metal chair with no arms on the front side of his desk while he circled to his side and sat in a similarly uncomfortable chair.

I twisted my fingers together and tapped my foot to try and release some nervous energy.

"I have some news about Allegra Odell's murder."

My eyes widened. "Okay."

"We found the murder weapon in a dumpster behind The Enchanted."

"Oh, that's great. I mean, not great, but…"

His upper lip twitched as I stumbled over my words. I couldn't look at him, so I focused on the back of a photo frame and wondered what picture it held.

He cleared his throat. "Would you like to see it?"

"The gun?" I waved my hands in front of me. "No thanks. I'm afraid of those things."

"The mugshot of the killer."

"I'm sorry, I must have missed something." Score a time out for not paying attention. I crossed my feet multiple times to release my growing anxiety.

His lips fluttered upward, and I swore I saw a little sparkle in his eye. "You did. I said we ran the prints on the gun, and they came back belonging to a Samuel Odell."

My eyes widened. "How did I miss that?"

He flipped the photo frame around and a black lab puppy smiled up from the photo. "I think you were trying to burn a hole through this frame, you were staring at it so intently."

A warmth crept up my chest, traveled to my neck and face, and heated them both well above room temperature. "I'm sorry. It's just been a long month."

"I can imagine."

"I would like to see the mugshot, yes. Samuel Odell is my uncle—was my uncle, but I've never met him."

The chief opened a file folder on his desk and handed me an eight by ten photo of an elderly man. I examined it closely. He had my mother's nose. I wondered if that was the case for Allegra, too. His silvery black hair, what my mother would have called salt and pepper, touched his shoulders in the back, and the sides covered his ears. He probably hadn't had a good haircut in months. He shared my mother's eyes, too, but his cheekbones were more chiseled, as was his chin, probably once pronounced, but less so having lost the battle with gravity.

He raised an eyebrow and adjusted his position on his chair. "You never met your aunt or uncle?" He used a slightly higher pitch to emphasize the *or.*

"No." I inhaled deeply and let the breath out slowly. "I'm finding out there's a lot about my family I didn't know."

His eyes softened, and a little butterfly nudged my stomach. I pointed my toes upward to distract it.

"I'm sorry. That must be hard."

I shrugged. "What's the saying? It is what it is."

He nodded once. "We've got a BOLO on your uncle. I'm concerned this has something to do with you or your mother's estate."

I chuckled to myself. If he only knew!

"If I could, I'd put someone on you, but I don't have that kind of manpower."

I blinked. "Excuse me?"

He leaned forward. "Ms. Odell—"

I waved my hand. "Please, call me Abby." I didn't mention that legally, I had a different last name, even though everyone referred to me as an Odell, even when I was married.

"Abby then. There's a reason for your estranged relatives to come to town at the time of your mother's," he paused, taking a deep breath before speaking again. "Passing. If we figure out that reason, we'll have a better chance of getting your uncle before he does something else."

If my uncle tried anything else, I feared Chief Ryder and a state full of law enforcement officers couldn't stop him. "I understand."

"That being said, is there something, perhaps in your mother's estate, that your relatives might want?"

I pictured my mother's A-frame house and went room through room, thanking the powers that be for my photographic memory, even though I knew the only thing of any use to my uncle was me, dead. "She really doesn't have anything of real value. The house is hers, it doesn't have a mortgage, but I can't imagine it's worth enough to kill for."

"You'd be surprised."

So would he, if he knew what good ol' Uncle Sammy was really after. "So, what am I supposed to do?"

"Keep your guard up, watch your back, and if you can, stay around public places for as long as possible. Being in a group is better than being alone. Do you have any weapons?"

"Weapons? This is Holiday Hills."

He smirked, opened a side drawer on his desk, and set out a little pink canister.

I stared at it.

"It's pepper spray." He lifted the key chain attachment. "You put it on your keys, and if need be, you spray it on an attacker. Here, let me show you."

He walked to my side of the desk and motioned for me to

stand. I did, my legs shaking a little. He put the small canister in my hand and used his to show me how to use it. His hand was big enough to cover mine, and the warmth of his touch sent little sparks of electricity through my skin. Positioned behind me, he leaned closer in, and I felt his warm breath on my neck. Peppermint. He smelled of peppermint, and a little pine too. I inhaled carefully, wanting to soak in the scent so I could pull it out of my memory later.

"You want to hit the eyes, so aim lower. Always aim lower. Even if you don't hit the eyes, the stuff will hurt. When you spray, immediately cut and run. It's going to get you, too, but if you aren't directly in its path, the effect is less." He lifted up my hand. "Like this." He pretended to hit the button on the canister, but I didn't realize he was only pretending and immediately yanked my hand from his, and flipped around, burying my head into his shoulder.

We both froze. Once I realized my mistake, I jerked away and bumped into his desk, sending a pile of file folders sailing to the ground.

"Oh my gosh!" I crouched down and began shoving the folders into a pile. "I'm so sorry." I didn't want to stand, worried he'd see my bright red face.

He bent down next to me and grabbed the pile of folders, smiling at me. "No worries." He chuckled as he stood. "Did you really think I'd spray?"

I shrugged. "I think I probably did."

When he smiled, little lines creased the corners of his eyes.

He handed me the spray. "I think you've got it."

I accepted it, sure my face was as bright a pink as the container. "May I ask why you have a bright pink thing of pepper spray in your desk?" My nose tickled, and I almost rubbed it, but didn't dare for fear something would happen.

He walked over to the drawer and pulled it open. "I keep a

stash of various colors for people I care about." He bit his lip. "And cases like this, of course."

"Of course."

He shut the drawer quickly and cleared his throat. "I'll be in touch as we progress in the investigation, and I'll check on you a couple times a day."

"You don't have to do that."

"I think I do." He took one of his business cards from a card holder on his desk and wrote something on the back of it. "My cell. If something happens, call 9-1-1, and if you can, call me right away. If you can't, I'll be there, but make sure to stay on the line with the operator or keep the phone connected. It helps us locate you."

His words concerned me. If the police chief thought I was in that much danger, given the magical factor at play, I knew it was even worse.

"In fact, may I have yours?"

Lost in the thought of magical danger, I hadn't paid attention to what he said. "My what?"

"Your cell phone number. I'd like to have it in case I need to get in touch with you." He removed his phone from his pocket. "I'll put you in my contacts."

A part of me wanted to jump for joy, but the other part knew it was all business.

* * *

The police department was just a few blocks from The Enchanted, so instead of driving, I'd walked over. I liked the crisp winter air; it refreshed and reawakened me even though it drained my skin of moisture in December. I ran into Peter Parallel on my way back.

"Hello, darling." Peter wore a black waist length coat with an attached hat hanging in the back. He wore a beanie to keep his balding head warm. "You out for a walk in this lovely winter weather?"

I smiled. "On my way back from a visit with the police chief." I fiddled with the can of pepper spray in my coat pocket.

"Parking tickets?"

I shook my head. "Did you know I have an aunt and uncle?"

He dropped his head, nodded slightly, then patted me on the shoulder. "How about we take a little walk together?"

I smiled. "I'd like that."

He lit a cigarette. I didn't even know he smoked. "In case you're wondering, I'm a warlock, but these days, I don't do much with magic. Just don't feel the need."

I wasn't surprised.

"I'm sure there's a lot for me to learn, but I'm hoping I won't have to really, I don't know, deal with it, I guess."

"You never know. It might come in handy a time or two."

"So far I've made it through life without it."

"Appears so. Your mom, she did right by you, wanting to give you a normal life and all. The magical world, well, it may be full of excitement but it's not always a good place either."

"I'm learning that."

"Your mom learned that, too, and the hard way. I'm not sure what you know and don't know."

"Bessie told me what happened to my father."

"Hmm. Janoah was a good man. It's too bad, what happened, but he died a hero, and you need to know that." He took a puff from the smelly cigarette and blew it out slowly. "But your mom, she never quite got over it, and when your granddaddy took Allegra and Samuel's powers, she didn't think that was enough. Even when your granddaddy banned them from town, she wasn't satisfied. She up and moved before you were born. It was just too much for her, I guess, out in the real world." He took another drag from his cigarette, then dropped it on the ground and smashed it with his boot. "It was hard for your mom, losing Janoah like that. I understood how she felt. I lost someone I loved, too. Never quite got over it."

"I'm sorry. I didn't know."

"Not many people know. We kept our relationship quiet. She wanted it to be a secret until the time was right, but that time never came."

"That must have been hard."

His eyes glossed over as he stared ahead. "You do what you got to do. Life goes on."

We'd circled the small old downtown area of Holiday Hills, all of three blocks, and at right about that time, stood in front of The Enchanted's door.

He held the door open for me. "Well, guess this is where we say goodbye."

"You're not coming in?"

"Nah, I've got some business to take care of. I'll be back in the morning like always. Can't miss a daily argument with Merlock, you know."

I gave the older man a hug. "Thank you."

He winked at me. "Any time, sweetie, any time."

I briefed Bessie on my conversation with Chief Ryder.

"A can of pepper spray? If he thinks someone is after you, why give you a can of that instead of something stronger?"

"You mean like mace?"

She nodded.

"I'm pretty sure it's not legal here in Georgia." I wiggled the can on my keychain. "Besides, do you really think any of this will help me?"

"You're right. You've got your own special kind of mace."

Cooper dragged himself from the chair in the display case and did his standard figure eights through my legs. I picked him up and put him on the table next to my laptop. He didn't speak,

not human style anyway, but he did purr, which, like other
Burmese cats, sounded like he had a sore throat. I always smiled
when he purred. I rubbed his ear, and he pressed the side of his
head into my hand, forcing me to rub harder. My nose itched,
and I swiped it with my free hand, sending Cooper flying across
the room and straight into a shelf of books. Thank God he
landed on his feet.

Bessie raised an eyebrow. "You might want to practice that."

"Or get my nose to stop itching. Seriously, I can't go through
life tossing things around every time my nose itches."

Cooper gave me the evil eye as he hopped back onto the table,
keeping a safe distance from my hand. I had a feeling his *slitted*
eyes and clicking sounds meant I owed him a can of tuna for
that.

"That'll stop eventually, just give it time. For now though,
there's things you can do to tone it down."

"Good, tell me."

She stood and stepped behind her counter, then handed me a
tea bag. "Here, put it in your coffee. It'll stop you from getting a
cold."

"But I don't have a cold."

"Just trust me on this, okay?"

I did as instructed.

Bessie went on as she pulled out the chair next to me and sat.
I hadn't noticed before, but she always faced the door when she
sat anywhere in the store.

"The good news is if Samuel had to use a human weapon to
kill Allegra, he probably doesn't have any powers."

"Cooper thinks that, too."

"Cooper? Your cat?"

I nodded.

"Well, look at that. You really are special."

"You already said that."

"Yes, I just didn't realize how powerful. Talking familiars are typically reserved for very powerful witches." She slid out of her chair and took something from behind the counter. She opened the small packet and dumped it into my coffee. "You're definitely going to need this."

I grimaced. "You're going to mess up the taste."

She laughed. "Don't worry about that. Anyway, talking cat, check. So, what did he tell you?"

She patted Cooper on the head. I waited for him to speak, but he just purred.

"He told me, among other things, a witch's powers could be stolen at the time of her death."

"Yes, that's true. But you just said he doesn't think Samuel has powers."

"Right."

She crossed her arms and uncrossed them as Merlock walked into the store. "You're back again?"

"Heat don't work at my place. It's cold. I could use a cup of coffee." He sat in his regular seat, and Mr. Charming flew over to the back of his chair. He picked at the man's head for a moment, made some funny grunting sound, and flew over to my table, perching on the seat next to me.

Bessie held up her finger my direction, then made Merlock his coffee.

She sat back down. "You were saying?"

"What if it was Allegra? What if she somehow found out my mom was sick and she took her powers?" I'd been stewing over that thought for a bit, but I hadn't quite worked through the details. "And Samuel found out, and he killed Allegra for them?"

"That would mean your grandfather's spell would have to have been broken for sure."

"Isn't anything possible in the magical world?"

"Well, to a certain degree, but I don't see how either one of them would have found you otherwise." She thought for a moment and then spoke. "Witches aren't psychics. The

Universe doesn't allow us to know everything, and we can't magically fix everything either. What's meant to be, what humans call fate, is going to be no matter what. Since some witches like to mess with that fate, whoever makes the decisions," she glanced upward, "up there, likes to keep us guessing."

"So, it' possible she could have found out then."

"It's possible that either Samuel or Allegra could have taken your mother's powers, yes."

"But wouldn't Mr. Charming know?"

"Mr. Charming's handsome," the bird said.

I smiled. "Yes, you are."

"Mr. Charming's handsome."

"Familiars only know what they're allowed to know, too."

I sunk in my seat. "This is complicated."

"That's life for you."

I made a mental note to stop making Esmerelda's magic so easily accessible. If real witches struggled, my fictional witch needed to, too.

* * *

I tried hard to use the *if I pretend there isn't a problem, there isn't a problem* theory on my new witchy life and the fact that someone was out for me so I could work on my novel. I spent hours instead, piddling on the internet learning as much as I could about my new world. I had no idea what was true and what wasn't, and I really shouldn't have used the internet as my professor, but my pickings were slim.

Bessie fed Cooper a can of tuna. She spoiled that cat terribly. She also gave Mr. Charming some fresh fruit, mostly chopped oranges and a few blueberries, and he sang as he ate. She set a ham and pimento cheese on wheat next to my computer, but it stayed there, untouched for another two hours. I stared at my laptop's background. A photo of my mother and I in The Enchanted, at my table, smiling for the camera. Mom's front teeth turned in slightly. She hated it, but I thought it made her extra pretty.

"Honey, it's late. I'm closing up, and you need to go home. Get some sleep, and we'll figure out what to do in the morning."

I forced my eyes out of stare mode and agreed. "I think I'm going to take a hot bath."

She'd tried to talk me into staying with her, but I refused.

"Then keep that pepper spray close by. You're not good with those powers yet, but hopefully that stuff will help you if you need it."

I barely got in the door and into my pajamas before I fell on the couch with a Hallmark Christmas movie lulling me to sleep. I dreamed Gabe Ryder was the love interest, a former business executive who'd come back to run the family ranch. I was the main character, a writer who'd gone to the ranch to write a love story featuring cowboys. The dream was beautiful until the tornado hit and blew the barn to pieces.

I snapped awake only to realize the tornado wasn't in my dream, it was in my apartment.

Cooper wrapped himself in and out of my legs. I rushed for Mr. Charming, who took off from his cage's perch and squawked and screamed as he flew around the funnel cloud whipping through my small apartment.

The funnel cloud headed straight for me, sucking up small tchotchkes from my shelves and whipping them at me. I swerved and ducked and a foot-tall snowman hit me on the shoulder. I screamed and charged into the two feet between me and the twirling mass, shoving my hands in front of me. "Get out of my apartment!" I shoved my hands toward it again. "Get out of my apartment!" The funnel cloud seemed to move backwards as I came at it, so I kept going, kept screaming, watched it deteriorate in front of me.

As my tchotchkes dropped haphazardly from the cloud, it formed into a dog like form, it's fur a blackish gray and beige. A wolf. It was a wolf. I picked up a large red candle and whipped it at the animal. "Get out of here!"

The candle hit the wolf on the left leg. He growled, showing me a set of massive, sharp white teeth.

I stepped backwards as the wolf came toward me. Cooper jumped into the air, his four paws stretched out in front of him, his teeny knife-like nails sticking out from his paws. He hissed and swatted at the wolf, attached himself to its head, and gnarled himself into a mass of cat and wolf fur I couldn't make out.

"Cooper, no!" I screamed and cried as the two animals fought, begging Cooper to stop, listening to him hiss and the wolf growl.

Mr. Charming flew over and somehow extracted Cooper from the mass of fur and tossed him toward me. The wolf stopped. We made eye contact, and then he spun in a circle, and disappeared in a cloud of dust.

A cloud of dust just like the one Merlock shifted into earlier.

CHAPTER 5

I called 9-1-1 and immediately regretted it. My apartment looked like a tornado hit it, which was basically true. The problem was, Holiday Hills wasn't struck by a tornado, so what was I going to tell the police? A wolf-like creature whipped up a major windstorm in my apartment just didn't seem like the right thing to say.

I rubbed my finger back and forth beneath my nose. "Uh, I… the…fix this!" I waved my hands over my head. "Please!"

Like a movie in reverse, every item in my house returned to its original spot. I watched in awe, as did Cooper and Mr. Charming.

"Addie's gone. Addie's gone," Mr. Charming said.

As if I needed the reminder. "I know, buddy." I stretched out my arm and he flew to it, squeezing his claws onto my forearm in what my mother used to call his death claw grip. The poor bird really missed our mom.

Chief Ryder pounded on my door. "Abby, it's Gabe. Let me in."

I unlocked the door, and Gabe and two other officers charged inside, hands on their guns, ready to do whatever it was police did when that kind of thing happened.

The chief's eyes bore into mine and then he quickly looked away. "Drew, take the bedroom. Scott, the kitchen."

The officers bolted to their respective territories.

"All clear," Scott yelled, then Drew followed suit.

Gabe's chest relaxed as he smiled the few inches down at me. "What happened?"

Thank God for my creative imagination. "An animal, maybe a coyote or something, got inside." I flipped around and faced my couch unable look him in the eye. "I'm sorry. I was scared, and I overreacted. I shouldn't have called 9-1-1."

He gripped my shoulder with a firm hand. "No, you did the right thing. Did you get a look at it?"

I nodded. "It was about the size of an, oh I don't know, maybe a German Shepherd? I'm not very good at this stuff. Blackish, with beige hair. Maybe it wasn't that big or maybe it was bigger." I rubbed the muscle between my shoulder and neck. "I really don't know. It happened so fast."

"We've had a couple coyote sightings recently. How'd it get in?"

I tipped my head back. "I don't know, I guess I left my door opened or something. Sometimes if I don't close it right it sort of pops back open."

He walked to the door, closed it, flipped the lock, and then yanked on the handle. "Feels secure to me. You might want to keep it locked, especially given the circumstances." He motioned for the other officers to leave. "I'll write up the report, don't worry about it."

They nodded as they left.

"Listen, you've got a lot going on." His eyes softened. "Maybe it's a good idea to stay with Bessie."

It might have been a good idea to him, but I needed to figure out how to deal with Samuel. I eyed the book from my mother's house on my small dining room table. Cooper must have noticed because he hopped up and stretched his little body over it. "I don't think Bessie could save me from a coyote attack."

"There's strength in numbers." Mr. Charming perched himself back onto his cage arm, and as he nibbled and picked at his feathers, Gabe walked over and rubbed his head. "Things have been tough for you, too, haven't they?"

My heart swelled into a beating ball of middle school girl love.

I kept my eyes on Cooper lying on the book. Not that Gabe would know what it was, but I didn't want any suspicion. "Thank you for coming. I'm sorry for making a big deal out of nothing."

He rubbed Mr. Charming's head one more time and walked the short distance back to me. "This wasn't nothing. The new home construction in the towns surrounding us creates a problem for their wildlife, and it ends up being our problem. We're working on solutions to rehome them, but it's not easy."

Rehoming whoever or whatever just entered my apartment wouldn't be easy either. "I can imagine." I stood there, twisting my fingers into a ball and staring at the floor.

"Well." He placed his hand on my shoulder. "Get some rest. I'll check on you in the morning."

When I looked up at him, his eyes were soft again. We stared at each other for a moment in that awkward, Hallmark movie kind of way, until he finally smiled and broke the connection.

I was both relieved and disappointed.

When he left, I fell onto the couch and groaned. "I'm never going to get used to this, am I?"

Cooper hopped off the book and sauntered over to the couch. He climbed up the side of it and sat next to me. "You'll figure it out. It just takes time."

"Is there a spell or something I can do that'll just, I don't know, fill me with witchy knowledge or something?"

He meowed. "Doesn't work that way. There's a lot we'll never know, but eventually we learn enough to get by."

"Get by? Great. That's exactly what I want. To get by."

"I'm sensing some sarcasm in your tone."

"You're sensing right." I ran my hand through my hair. "What am I supposed to do? I can't just sit here and let this stuff happen."

"No, you can't. First off, you should cast a protection spell over your house. That'll keep stuff like that from happening again."

"What's second?"

He licked his foot. I never realized how much that cat licked himself. It was awkward, waiting for him to finish so he could answer my question. The fact that I waited for him to answer my question, with a human voice, was obviously awkward too. No. More like surreal.

My entire life was surreal.

"I don't have a second."

"You're not all that helpful."

"Hey, I attacked that thing."

My eyes widened. I'd totally forgotten that. What an awful cat slash familiar mom I was. I picked him up and held him in front of me, examining his tiny brick of a body for injuries. "I'm so sorry. I don't know how I could forget that."

His face contorted into a grimace. "You've got a lot on your mind."

I rotated him to the left and then to the right, checking and rechecking him for cuts or bites or whatever that thing might have done.

He squeezed out of my grip and landed on the coffee table. "I'm fine. I'm fine. You don't have to get all weird about it. It's my job."

"Right. My talking cat's telling me not to get all weird about something. There's no irony in that at all."

I had no ideas cats could shrug.

"Listen, it's going to take a while for you to adjust to all this, and I get that." He climbed off the coffee table and headed for the small dining room table. "But this will help." He shoved the book with a paw, and it teetered on the edge of the table.

"Hey!" I rushed over and grabbed the book before it fell. "You might hurt it."

"You have no clue what the thing's been through. It'll survive a little fall."

I carried it carefully back to the couch. "Still, I don't want to take any chances." I set it down on the coffee table and stared at it, waiting for it to do something.

It did something alright. It sat there like a normal book.

I looked over at Cooper. "It's not doing anything."

He hopped from table to table.

"Woah, for a cat with such little legs, that's impressive."

"Don't judge. I can do things you can't even imagine."

"You should be a writer. You've got this irony thing down."

"I'm a talented kitty."

The book flipped open and page after page turned rapidly in front of us. I gasped. I didn't think I'd ever get used to living a life I believed to be fictional. When it stopped, Cooper stretched his head over the pages it landed on and pawed at the one closest to him.

"This one."

I furrowed my brow. "How do you know? You said you can't read."

"I just know. Trust me."

I read the spell. "Huh. You're right."

"Usually am."

Great. A snarky talking cat. As if I should have expected something else.

"You going to read it?"

"I did. It says I need a candle."

He hopped over to my small TV entertainment center and swatted a candle off the top. "Here."

"Hey! Stop that."

"Cats like to shove things off tables. It's our jam."

I shook my head. "You're really coming into your own, aren't you?"

"I've been my own man for over a hundred years. You're just meeting the real me."

"Over a hundred years?"

He stood up on his hind legs and stretched his front paws out, flipping them from side to side. "I'm in pretty good shape, right? Still got me some muscles."

I rolled my eyes and picked up the candle, digging into the little cabinet on the entertainment center for a lighter. I lit the candle and set it on the coffee table next to the book and read the spell out loud.

"Protect this space, from danger or harm, fill it with love, purpose and charm. Wrap it in white light, and prepare it to fight."

The room lit up like a summer thunderstorm in Georgia. I pushed myself into the back of the couch, afraid of what was happening, of what might come.

The lights stopped, and my room was exactly as it had been, except for a dozen roses in a vase on my dining room table. Cooper and I both stared at it.

He smelled the pretty flowers. "They smell nice."

"Weird."

"Spells get a little wonky sometimes. Witchcraft isn't a perfect science."

"Great." My nose itched. I scratched it, and another vase full of roses appeared. "Woah, I wasn't thinking about that."

"You were thinking about roses. Told you, it's tricky for a newbie." He slipped his paw behind the first vase and looked at me.

I pointed my finger at him. "Don't you dare."

He drew the paw back. "Sorry, I'm a cat. It's in my nature." He hopped off the table.

I eyed the book, taking note of my flannel pajamas. "When do you think I'm going to be ready?"

"Ready for what?"

"To face whatever it is that's trying to take away my powers."

"When the universe says you're ready. I can't tell you when that'll be."

The book's pages whipped to almost the last page.

I watched in awe. It would never get old. "Isn't there any order to this thing?"

"You get what you get."

"Apparently." I read the pages it opened to. "I guess I'm ready."

Cooper meowed.

I pointed to the right page of the book. "It's not exactly a spell, it's more like instructions."

"To do what?"

"What I wanted to do before, locate the thing trying to hurt me."

He scrutinized the page carefully, aiming his little paw at a specific sentence. "What's this say?"

"I need a crystal or something on a string, and a map."

He sat next to the book. "Yup, it's doing a locating spell."

"Who has a map? I have GPS on my phone."

"Yeah, that's not gonna work." He eyed my nose. "Well?"

"Well what?"

He eyed my nose again.

Without thinking, I touched it, and a map and crystal necklace appeared on the table. "Woah."

"Cool, huh?"

I had to admit, it was. I also had to admit I really didn't know how to read a map. I did what the book instructed, held the crystal over the large paper and watched it swing all on its own. Esmerelda would definitely get herself a swinging crystal.

It stopped swinging and stuck its point onto a spot on the map. I watched in disbelief, though I really shouldn't have been surprised. Considering what I'd seen over the past few days, nothing should have been a surprise, but it was.

Cooper stood on the map, his head close to the crystal. "What's it at?"

I examined it carefully, realizing it wasn't all that hard to read after all.

"My mother's house."

His eyes widened.

I dropped the crystal and jumped off the couch. "We have to go." I headed for the door, and as I grabbed my coat, noticed my flannel pajamas again. "Crap." I rushed to my bedroom to change, tangling myself up in the arms of my sweatshirt as I tried to pull it over my head. "Darn it."

"Hold up there, partner," he said, standing on the closest pair of jeans. "You don't know if this spell is locating the person coming after you. How many times do I have to tell you this stuff is tricky? For all we know, it could be locating an earring you lost ten years ago. Just because it's pointing to your mother's house, doesn't mean it's what you think."

That stalled me a bit, but I shoved him off my jeans and shimmied into them.

My eyes widened. "Yeah, right, but it doesn't mean it isn't, either." I snatched my keys off the dresser and we headed out, Mr. Charming closing in on our backs.

It wasn't a far drive to my mother's, and I pulled over a few streets before hers and parked near a row of trees. I didn't know what this thing could or couldn't do, and I didn't want it knowing I was close. Of course, if it was Samuel, and he had taken my mother's powers from either my mother or Allegra, he could have probably figured it out, so the least I could do was make it harder for him.

Mr. Charming squawked as we climbed out of the car.

I checked my cell phone. It was after midnight. How had that happened? "Hush, we don't want to wake anyone."

Not a single house had an interior light on. Most of them were decorated for the holiday season, their yards filled with plastic or lit deer and snowmen, their windows beautifully colored with white and multi-colored lights. Holiday Hills residents did the holiday season right, and I couldn't help but wonder if maybe the whole Santa Claus thing was true, too.

I'd walked the area millions of times, taking the short cut from my house to a friend's down the street or just into town. I knew the quickest way to my mom's, but I didn't want to walk between homes and set off alarms. We weren't the most technologically advanced town, but the Ring doorbell wasn't too complicated, and the last thing I needed were phones beeping with motion near their doors alerting residents to my seemingly shady activities.

The last house on the back street sold a few weeks before. I knew the owners, and I knew they'd already moved, so I headed to it, thinking we'd go through its yard. We'd have to cut through the house behind it, too, but better to risk only one house than an entire block.

"Addie's here. Addie's here." Mr. Charming planted himself on my shoulder.

"Zip it, bird," I whispered.

"Zip it, bird. Zip it, bird."

"That worked," Cooper said.

"Zip it, cat."

"Duly noted."

The light in the back of the vacant house popped on. We froze. It wasn't vacant after all.

"Oh, crap."

The back door flew open and a tall man stepped out. "Who's there?"

I'd grown to know that voice well over the past few days. Oh crap, oh crap, oh crap.

"Addie's here. Addie's here."

I pinched Mr. Charming's beak together.

"We're busted," Cooper said. He took off for the trees at the far end of the yard.

"Great, thanks," I whispered.

"Abby, is that you?" Gabe Ryder sauntered over, his flashlight beaming in my eyes.

I squinted and held my hand up. Mr. Charming flew off me and landed on a covered chair on the patio. "Chief, yeah, uh, it's me."

He held the light up toward the sky, and the shadow of it remained burned into my corneas for a few seconds. "What're you doing? It's after midnight."

I twisted my fingers together. "I'm sorry. I didn't mean to alarm you, I just couldn't sleep. We're out for a walk." Really Abby? That's what you could come up with in a pinch?

Cooper sauntered over and rubbed circles between my stiff legs.

"A walk? Through my backyard?"

"I, uh, I thought the owners moved out."

"The old ones did and then I moved in."

My eyes adjusted, and I saw the combination confused and concerned look on his face. "I'm sorry. I didn't know."

"Police chiefs don't usually send out relocation announcements."

"I would think not."

"It's cold out here, why don't you come in? I'll grab my keys and drive you home. That parrot's got to be freezing."

"Oh, really, it's okay. We can walk. He likes the crisp air."

"Bye, bye Addie. Bye, bye Addie," Mr. Charming said.

"I insist." Gabe chuckled. "Don't criticize my décor. The movers were just here today, and I've only unpacked two boxes so far. It'll probably take me a year to get the rest done, even though I only have about fifteen.

He was right, he didn't have a lot of boxes, and the one in the kitchen he did unpack obviously contained a coffee pot and cups, because other than two empty beer bottles, those were the only things on his counter.

"I love what you've done with the place."

He smiled and took his keys off the counter as Mr. Charming flew into the hallway.

"Mr. Charming, get back here."

Gabe went down the small hallway after him and returned with the bird on his shoulder. "I think he likes me."

My heart picked up its pace.

"It looks like he does. I'd give him to you, but he's been around a long time. He's family."

"Oh, I wasn't trying to—" I smiled, and he smiled too. "You were joking."

I was kind of surprised at how comfortable I was starting to feel around him. "I was."

"I'll remember that."

"Oh, that sounds a little scary," I said, my mouth rounding into a smile full of teeth. My face warmed, and I knew my cheeks were pink.

He walked toward the door, but I didn't want the ride home. I needed to get to my mother's and quick. Darn him and his cuteness for making me forget my mission.

"Um, you know, on second thought, I was headed to my mom's place, and I'd still like to go by there, so you don't need to drive us back. I hate putting you out anyway."

"I can take you to your mom's house. It's a block away, right?"

He'd done his homework. "Yes, but really, I like the crisp air, and this is Holiday Hills, I don't think anything's going to happen to me." I removed my keys from my pocket and wiggled the pepper spray canister. "Besides, a wise man gave me an excellent weapon."

He narrowed his eyes. "I'm not comfortable letting you walk at night like this. You're several blocks from your place, and we haven't located your uncle."

I didn't want him to know my car was down the street. "Yes, I know. I may just stay at my mom's for the night. Really, it's fine."

"I'm not going to change your mind, am I?"

"Nope, sorry Chief."

"I could arrest you."

That sentence sounded like it was filled with double, maybe even triple, meanings. He'd totally stumped me. I didn't know what to say. "Uh, well, I, um…"

He laughed. "I'm kidding. Just do me a favor. Send me a quick text when you get to your mom's, okay?"

"Yes, sir. I promise."

"I'm not that much older than you, please don't call me sir."

I blushed again. "You got it, Chief." Dear Lord.

He smiled and walked me back behind his house. "I'm going to stand here until I can't see you anymore."

"That'll be quick. It's dark out."

"True, but I've got great night vision."

I shook my head and headed through the neighbor's yard, feeling his eyes on me the entire way.

My heart raced as I approached my mother's house, and it wasn't because of the flirtatious interaction with the police chief. Cooper rushed ahead of us and disappeared into the darkness.

Great, I thought. Just what I needed, my protective kitty to bolt when things got interesting.

Mr. Charming dug his claws into my shoulder. "Addie's gone. Addie's gone. Bye, bye Addie."

I hoped he'd tire of repeating the constant reminder of our loss soon.

"Yes, buddy. I know. I miss her, too."

I tiptoed through the side yard, quietly making my way to the back porch, where the windows didn't have large shrubs beneath them. The house was dark, but what did I expect of a warlock who wasn't supposed to be there? Every light in the house shining brightly? I peeked through the first window, but it was too dark to see anything other than the outlines of the kitchen table. I watched for movement but saw nothing.

I snuck carefully over to the other window, trying hard not to make a sound. Mr. Charming mumbled something, and I told him to hush, which, for a change, he did. My cell phone beeped with the familiar sound of Stella's notification. I quickly hit the button to silence the sound and switched it to silent. I read Stella's message.

"Hey, Dad got in a car accident this evening. He's fine, just a sprained ankle. I'm heading there for a bit to get him settled. I'll be back tomorrow I'm sure."

I responded with a short, "Give him a kiss for me."

My mother's bedroom was dark except for a dim, barely noticeable light in her closet. Its soft glow scarcely showing under the door frame. If anyone—other than me—walked through her back yard, they wouldn't have noticed it, unless—like me—they stuck their head up close to her window.

I knew the light hadn't been on before. I'd gone through the house and made sure every light was off before I left, so either someone was there or had been there. I flattened my back against her house, my breathing short and quick. What was I supposed to do? The book hadn't given me any insight on that, and I'd stupidly just rushed off to come here and do what? Use my magical powers on someone or something?

What was I thinking? Where had my rational thought gone? Right out the window with my version of reality, that's where. Everything was new to me, my powers, the magical world, my talking cat, the additional family, the threat against my life. As if

I'd been able to really think clearly since my mother died anyway.

Cooper showed up and rubbed himself through my legs. "It's all clear. No one's here."

"What should I do?" I asked my cat.

"Breathe."

"Great. I think I can handle that much." I breathed in deeply, forcing my lungs to relax even though my hands shook. I crouched down, picked him up, and held him in front of the window, keeping my body glued to the house. "The light in the closet is on."

"Okay?"

"I didn't leave it on."

"Well, whoever did is gone."

I yanked him back and held him level with my face. "How do you know?"

"Really?"

I wasn't sure what I was supposed to say. "Yes, really."

"I'm your familiar, I know things."

"Are you sure?"

"Really?"

"Stop that. I'm new to this."

"Good point. I'll cut you some slack. Yes, I'm sure. Could you please put me down? I feel a little exposed with my legs dangling like this."

I grimaced and set him on the ground.

"Not that you can see anything, but now that our relationship has changed, it's a little weird to be left so, you know, naked like this sometimes."

"A little?" I peeked into the window again. "What should we do?"

"Go back to the car. I'm tired, and the bird is cold."

"But what about the light?"

"Like I said, whoever left it on is gone."

We took a longer route back to my car just in case Gabe decided to hang outside and see if we cut through his yard again.

I started the engine and kicked the heat up, but since we weren't far from home, it barely heated by the time we got to my place. I parked out front, on the side of the road in front of The Enchanted instead the back alley where I usually kept my car overnight. As I got out of my car, a dog stepped into view under a streetlight a few feet away.

I jerked back when I realized it wasn't a dog, but a wolf, and one that looked awfully similar to the one I'd seen in my house. Awfully similar to Merlock Dupe. I grabbed my pepper spray and held it out in front of me. Mr. Charming flew toward The Enchanted and sat in front of the locked door. Cooper stood in front of me, bracing himself for another fight, claws out and hissing loudly at the animal.

A cloud of dust appeared, filling up the space surrounding it. As quickly as the dust appeared, it disappeared, leaving Merlock Dupe standing naked in front of me.

We stared at each other, our mouths open wide, and me doing everything possible not to look where I really didn't want to, but my eyes kept angling that way anyway. I covered them and dropped my head toward the ground. "Oh my gosh!"

"Uh, oh." He rushed behind another parked car, one that belonged to the man who lived in the apartment above the pharmacy next to The Enchanted. "I'm so sorry. I was...I uh...I... sometimes this happens."

I kept my eyes covered. "It's okay, you don't have to explain."

"Give me a minute. Don't look."

"Don't have to worry about that."

I heard footsteps run off, but I kept my eyes covered. I didn't know what to do. If I uncovered them, I might see something that could scar me for life—that wasn't a joke—but I didn't want to stand there much longer.

The steps returned. "Okay, we're good."

I cracked my fingers open just a touch and saw a pair of pants. When I uncovered my eyes completely, he was just finishing pulling a shirt over his head. His feet were bare.

"Oh, dear God all mighty, I did not need to see that," Cooper said. He dropped down onto four paws and sat between my legs.

I glared at the old man. "What's going on?"

"I'm a shifter, this is what I do." The matter of fact tone of his voice implied he ran through town shifting into wolf form on a regular basis even though I recalled Bessie saying he scared people sometimes.

I held onto my pepper spray for dear life and flung my other hand in the air and waved it. "You, you…run around naked at night?"

"Well, not really. Wolves have hair, so I'm not actually naked."

"Until you shift back to your human form."

"Like I said, it happens sometimes. Besides, you weren't supposed to see that."

"Yet you did it in front of me anyway."

"You looked scared. I don't like scaring people, and you're a new witch, so I was worried. I wasn't paying attention to what I was doing, so I forgot my clothing."

Wow, Merlock actually tried to be considerate. "Thanks, I guess. Maybe next time though you should just run around the corner or something?"

He dropped his head. "Maybe."

"It's late. Don't you think you should get home?"

"I could say the same thing to you."

I shifted my feet, relaxing the death grip I had on the canister. "I couldn't sleep."

"It's not good for a witch to be out alone like this, especially a new one like you. You don't know what could happen."

He stepped closer to me, and suddenly the unassuming old man sent shivers up my spine. I didn't like the implied threat behind his words. "I can handle myself." I tightened my grip around my canister of pepper spray again.

"'Course you can. If you're anything like your momma, you're a force to be reckoned with. Wouldn't be easy, coming after you."

Cooper's little body stiffened at my feet.

I blinked, trying hard to keep from shivering. "Okay then. I'm going to bed. Have a nice, uh, stroll." I walked straight past him and ducked quickly around the back of the building to get to my apartment, both Cooper and Mr. Charming at my side. I flattened my back onto the rough bricks and breathed quietly through my nose. Mr. Charming hovered nearby.

"Shh," I told him.

He floated to the ground and stood still like me.

Cooper kept close to my feet. "I don't feel good about this."

I kept my pepper spray tight in my hand against the wall. Not that it could harm a shapeshifter, but it was all I had. Other than a gift of magic I'd yet to understand. "I just want to see what he's going to do," I whispered.

We watched Merlock on the sidewalk, examining his surroundings by the soft glow of the streetlamp. A small funnel of wind circled around his bare feet, and I gasped as his bony toes lengthened, grew hair and nails, and he morphed into the claws of a dangerous animal. An animal who preyed on the weak.

"This isn't good," Cooper said.

Merlock the man disappeared. He'd warped into his wolf form, and even though I stood there scared, unsure, and fascinated, I made mental notes of what I saw, thinking I could one day use them in my Esmerelda books.

When you're a writer, your mind never stops, especially at the most inappropriate times.

The wolf growled. I pushed my back harder into the tough bricks and held my breath. I didn't want him to know we were there. He slinked our direction, his prowl cautious and severe, ears up on his low head.

"Oh, sh—"

"Shh," I hissed at my cat who'd obviously spent too much time around my best friend with the foul mouth.

Merlock froze, a foot raised mid step.

Cooper went up on his hind legs and hissed as Merlock pounced our direction. I panicked, raising my hands and spraying the pepper spray as the wolf charged toward us. Cooper hissed, the spray not at all affecting him. Just as Merlock's feet landed only inches from us, his sharp, pointed teeth bared in a snarl, I screamed, "Go away!"

The wolf vanished in a puff of smoke.

I stood in sheer disbelief, staring as the cloud of smoke disappeared, the spot where Merlock once stood bare.

Cooper pushed his body into my leg. "Uh, good job, but we gotta get out of here, Ab."

I shook my head, clearing the fog of confusion mixed with a whole lot of adrenaline. "Yeah, let's…let's go."

We scurried to the very back of the building. I jammed my key into the lock, flung the door open, and we all rushed inside and up to my apartment, where I did the same thing. I slammed my door, flipped the locks, and leaned against it, panting like a dog.

Cooper jumped onto my small dining table. "Whatever's in that bottle is useless. Where'd you get it anyway?"

I plucked the pepper spray from my pocket and set it on the table. "The police chief gave it to me for protection."

Cooper laughed. "From what? Bugs?"

I furrowed my brow. "It's pepper spray. It keeps attackers away."

"Apparently, not the magical kind."

He had a point.

"You need to focus on using your powers to protect and defend yourself instead of the traditional ways."

I walked into the kitchen with my head held high. "I did use my powers, and I'm pretty darn proud of myself for it."

He laughed again. "By accident, yeah."

Having a talking cat was one thing but having a talking cat that found enjoyment in mocking me was another.

"Do you think it was Merlock in my mom's house? Could he be the one after me?"

"Why would an old shapeshifter come after you?"

"Maybe he was the one that killed my father. No one's ever mentioned what happened to them. Just that my aunt and uncle were banished."

"Merlock can't be the shifter that killed your dad, Ab."

"Why not?"

"Because your grandfather hunted them down and killed them both."

I closed my eyes for a moment, letting that sink in. "I guess not then." I put a pot of water on for chamomile tea and then got ready for bed. It was late, and I was tired, and I didn't need or want to think about attacking shapeshifters or talking cats or even pepper spray. I needed sleep. Heavenly, REM sleep.

CHAPTER 6

*B*essie filled my cup with steaming hot coffee. It smelled slightly burnt, but she'd assured me it wasn't. "He what? That doesn't sound like Merlock."

"It was unnerving." I added a splash of cream and sipped. "Oh, this is good." I played it off like it was more a nuisance than terrorizing. I didn't want Bessie worried any more than she already was.

She smiled. "Thank you. It's got a pinch of toad feet in it. That's what gives it the burnt smell. Charbroiling the toad is a pain, but it's worth it."

My mouth dropped open. I set the cup down and stared at it as my stomach churned.

Bessie laughed. "I'm kidding. It's the vanilla. I don't charbroil toads. That kind of thing only happens in your books, sweetie."

I breathed in and picked up the cup once again. "That was mean."

Her smile grew, engulfing the bottom half of her face. "It's always fun to pick on the new witches."

I narrowed my eyes at her. "Careful or I'll make you disappear in a cloud of smoke, too."

She sat at the table with me, her smile gone and her eyebrow raised as if to say, *good luck with that.* Neither Merlock nor Peter had come into the store yet.

"There was something strange in the air last night. I'll give you that. But for Merlock to come at you, that's highly inappropriate. He's been warned about that kind of behavior, too. He must have had a really bad day."

Inappropriate wasn't the word I'd choose, but it wasn't the time to debate adjectives. "The little nudge I'm getting telling me it's not Samuel coming after me is getting stronger by the minute."

She chewed on the side of her lip. "Oh honey, you can't think it's Merlock? He's harmless."

"He sure didn't look harmless last night."

Mr. Charming chirped away on Merlock's chair and then broke into the Eagles "There's a New Kid in Town" chorus, his impression of Glenn Frey disturbingly accurate. We watched him for a second like we did every time he sang a song from my mother's favorite band.

"Anyway, Merlock can't take your powers. He's a shifter. It's like trying to breed a cat and a dog. It's just not possible."

"Then why act all passive aggressive, threatening and then come after me like that?"

She sighed. "Like I said, he was probably having a bad day. Lord knows he's done things like that before, just not in a while."

I tilted my head. "What do you mean?"

Cooper hopped onto the table and stood on his hind legs. It amazed me how he could balance himself like that. Pretty talented cat.

"Coop, off." I picked him up and plopped him onto the floor, but he jumped back onto the table again, ears up and claws out.

He stared at the front door. Bessie turned to see what had him on the defense, and I focused on the door, my muscles tightened, ready to jump from my seat and defend myself, waiting for it to blow open with someone or something ready to attack me.

A white light flashed and blew by outside, but that was it. Cooper's stiff body relaxed. He dropped back to all fours and crawled off the table, settling next to my feet on the floor.

"That was weird," I said.

Bessie shrugged. "Magic is everywhere in Holiday Hills. You get used to that kind of thing."

"As if."

"You will, I promise."

"What were you saying about Merlock?"

"Oh," she waved her hand like it was nothing. "He just got into a bit of trouble years back." She nodded her head and pressed her lips together. "Well, it was more than nothing. He got in an argument and it almost got him kicked out of town, but it was settled."

"An argument? With whom?"

"Your mother."

My eyes widened. "What could he possibly argue about with my mom?"

"You know, I never did get an answer to that, from either of them. Addie said it wasn't anything important, and Merlock, he was too ashamed to discuss it, considering he was on probation here and all."

"Probation?"

She nodded. "He turned into his wolf form and stayed that way for days, stalking around town and scaring everyone. Holiday Hills residents don't do that, they aren't allowed to do that, and he knew it. Instead of banning him, the council voted to put him on probation. We knew he was cranky, always had been, but generally, he's harmless." She sipped her coffee. "I really think he was probably just having a bad day and decided to take it out on you."

Peter Parallel walked in, smiling as always. But that smile

dropped and adverted to a frown when he set his eyes on me. He walked over and placed his hand on my shoulder. "How you doin', kiddo?"

I patted his hand. "I'm fine, Peter. Thank you for asking."

"You sure? You look a little worse for the wear."

Bessie stood and he sat with me as she prepared him a cup of coffee.

"Something strange happened last night." I glanced at Bessie. She touched her finger to her lips. I waved my hand and shook my head. "But it's nothing, really. I'm fine."

Bessie handed him the coffee. He took a sip and thanked her. "I like the vanilla."

She smiled and shifted her eyes toward me. "It's charbroiled toad."

I rolled my eyes.

Peter laughed. "She get you with that one? It's her favorite. She's been doing it for years. Careful. She's got a few other ones up her sleeve." He winked at me. "Keep an eye on her. She's a feisty one."

The door opened, and Merlock walked in. Cooper positioned himself in front of my table like one of those guards with the big fuzzy hats protecting the Queen of England. Mr. Charming chirped from the old man's chair. Merlock grunted something and sat as we all stared at him.

I leaned toward Peter and whispered, "Is he okay?"

Peter examined him from the short distance. "Looks like he had a rough night." He flicked his head toward Bessie. "Haven't seen this since that last time."

She nodded, acting like we hadn't just discussed it. "Kind of does, doesn't he? Hope he's okay." She poured Merlock a cup of coffee but didn't walk over to him in the seat. "This is a bookstore, not a café."

Merlock glanced at her as she held up the cup.

"You want it? You got to come and get it."

He pushed himself from the chair and limped toward the counter, grunting first a frustrated sound, then something that matched his limp.

"He's limping," I whispered.

Peter stood. "You okay there, Merlock?"

Merlock grunted again. "Yeah, yeah. I'm fine."

He wouldn't look me in the eye. "Couldn't sleep last night. Went out for a walk, and I don't know, something happened."

Peter eyed him up and down. "Happened? You fall and sprain your ankle or something?"

"Something attacked me. Just came out of nowhere and jumped me. I fought it, it was strong. A lot stronger than me. I'm hurting bad."

Bessie lowered her voice to nearly a whisper. "Something attacked you?"

Merlock rubbed the back of his neck. "I think I injured it, but I'm not sure." He held up his hand and flipped it over, squinting his eyes as he examined his palm. "I'm battered and beaten up, but I'm still standing, so that's a good thing."

Bessie rushed around the counter and held his hand in hers. It was a gentle, almost motherly gesture. "It's all torn up." She hurried back around the counter and wet a small cloth. "Here. Press this on it. I've got some hydrogen peroxide in back. Let me get that. You're going to need some Band-Aids, too." She dashed to the back of the store and disappeared into the back room.

I stared at Cooper, and if I didn't know better, I would have sworn he shrugged. Could I have done that to Merlock? Could my magic have injured him? If so, why wouldn't Merlock just say so? Why make up a story and not even look at me? No, I thought, it couldn't have been me. Merlock wasn't the type of person to avoid an argument or blame someone for his unhappiness. If I'd done it, he'd have said so outright, I'm sure of it.

"Did you get a look at it?"

"That's the thing." Merlock leaned against the counter,

stretching out his arm and resting his hand palm up. "Whatever it was looked just like me."

As Merlock told the story of his attack—still not making eye contact with me—both Bessie and Peter tried to make sense of it. I listened, eyed Cooper a few times, but he kept his mouth shut. Mr. Charming sat on Merlock's shoulder, picking at his hair. Merlock didn't even push the parrot away once. He really wasn't himself. Everything about him felt off, strange, and even though he said he'd been attacked, it didn't feel right to me. He hadn't once looked at me. Did he think it was me? Did he think I came back and attacked him as retribution or something for his odd behavior when we'd talked? He couldn't. Well, I guess he could, but he'd be wrong. Attack aside, Merlock Dupe wasn't acting like himself, and that kept the hairs on the back of my neck standing at attention.

The door opened and Gabe walked in. Merlock's shoulders curved inward, and he stopped talking about the incident. Bessie and Peter eyed him and then Gabe, and then Bessie got up to make the chief a cup of coffee.

Was Merlock hiding something, and did they see it, too?

"Got another new brew," she said, handing Gabe the cup. "If you don't like it, I'll make a pot of the regular stuff."

He smiled and sipped the steaming liquid. "Hmm. Vanilla?"

Why could everyone taste that but me? Or did vanilla just taste like broiled toad?

Merlock stood, noticed his pant leg stuck in his boot, and adjusted it. He straightened again, and squeezed his shoulder blades together, holding his injured hand at his side. I watched him carefully, but he still wouldn't look me in the eye. "Thanks for the coffee, but I got to go," he said. He limped toward the door and left.

I leaned toward Peter and whispered, "That was odd."

"Do me a favor, keep your distance from him until he's back to normal, okay?"

I nodded quickly. "Trust me, that will not be a problem."

Gabe stepped over and greeted us both with a slight nod. He exchanged pleasantries with Peter, talked about football, mentioning something about half sacks and eligible receivers, losing me at the mention of the sport. I set up my computer while they boy-talked, and Bessie straightened up a shelf of books. Mr. Charming flew over to his regular perch on the old leather chair and picked at his feathers. Cooper sauntered over to the chair in the display and settled in for a day of intense napping.

Everything felt completely normal and entirely different at the same time.

"Abby, I have some news."

I glanced up at Gabe. "News? About my aunt?"

"Can we talk?"

Peter stood. "I've got a busy day ahead, so I'm going to head out." He nodded at me and gave me a quick wink.

Bessie kept herself busy reorganizing a bookshelf in the far corner of the store.

"We got a call late last night. Hunters found a body in the woods in Cumming."

"And they called Holiday Hills?" I knew enough to know that meant something I probably wouldn't like.

"We'd put a BOLO out on your uncle. When Forsyth County got to the scene, they found an ID and—"

My chest sank. "It was my uncle." Which meant either it wasn't my uncle coming after me, or someone got to him before he could finish the job. But who?

He nodded once. "I'm sorry."

I blinked and shook my head. "No, don't be sorry. I have no emotional connection to that man. So, what does this mean for my aunt?"

He released a breath. "Forsyth County found bullet shells that matched the ones at the cemetery. Looks like your aunt's murder's been solved."

"May I ask what happened to my uncle?"

"Cumming's had a problem with coyotes. They think a pack of them came up on your uncle's camp and surprised him."

"Are you sure it's coyotes? Could it have been wolves?"

He raised an eyebrow. "Wolves? In Cumming? Northern Georgia hasn't had wolves since the early 90s."

Maybe the kind that weren't magical. "Oh, I had no idea."

"Coroner wanted you to come identify the body, but I told him you'd never met Samuel. He'd still like to meet with you though."

I tilted my head. "Did he say why?"

"You're the next of kin, so both your aunt and uncle's final arrangements are left to you."

I blanched. "What? No, I...I wouldn't...I wouldn't know what to do. I didn't even know them."

"I know, but it's how things work. You don't have to have funerals, but you do need to decide what you want done."

I had no idea what I wanted done, or what should be done. A part of me felt bad, but for the most part, I didn't care. I was relieved. If Samuel had been the one trying to get my powers, then that was over. Things would go back to normal. Well, a new normal anyway, and I wouldn't have to worry about a threat I barely understood. Unless it wasn't Samuel that wanted my magic.

"Abby?"

I blinked. "Oh, yeah. I guess I should do that."

"I've got some free time today. If you want, I'll go with you."

"No, it's okay. I can handle it." I'd never been to the coroner's office, and I didn't even know where it was. "I'm going to need the address though."

He smiled. "I'll text it to you."

"Thank you. Chief, do they know why he was camping in the woods?"

"My guess is there was less of a chance of being identified that way."

"That makes sense."

"I'll give the coroner a call and tell him you'll be by later today."

"That would be great." I pointed to my computer. "I'm behind on this manuscript, but I'll make time to go there. Better to get this done and move on."

He smiled. I liked his smile. Little lines sprouted from the corners of his eyes, and it was sexy. "You get to that, and like I said, if you want me to go with you, I'm free."

The door burst open, and Stella walked in, bellowing the lyrics to a song I'd never heard.

Gabe smiled despite her inability to carry a tune.

Bessie plugged her ears and shook her head. "For the sake of my hearing, please stop."

Stella saw Gabe and froze, mouth open. Her eyes traveled from Gabe to me. She nodded slowly, but I laughed to distract Gabe from seeing her nonverbal communication directed at me. "My ears. They'll never be the same."

"Oh my gosh. I didn't know you were here," she said, her eyes locked on Chief Ryder.

He pointed at himself. "She's talking to me I presume?"

"I think so," I said.

Stella's face was as red as her cherry red sweater. "I am so embarrassed."

Gabe laughed. "Your voice is, uh, entertaining."

I swallowed hard. "That's a nice way of saying it."

She marched over to the table and tossed her bag on a chair. "Some people think my voice is music to their ears."

"Tone deaf people," Bessie said.

"I'm with her," I said.

Gabe laughed. "On that note." He smiled at me and said, "I'll give the coroner a call," as he headed toward the door.

Stella prepared her own cup of coffee, claiming she had some magic powder to add to it.

If she only knew.

She sat at the chair and set up her mobile office, her laptop, a notebook, and a manuscript in a binder. "So, look at you, getting all comfy and cozy with the police chief."

"We weren't getting anything, and I thought you were at your dad's?"

"I was. He's the crankiest patient I've ever dealt with in my life. Not that I've ever dealt with any patients, but still. Kicked me out, said he could take care of himself."

"So you left? I thought he'd hurt himself?"

She nodded as she sipped her coffee. "Yup, but the old man's stubborn as a mule. Didn't want me helping him. Said I had my own life and he'd take care of himself." She whistled. "Saw a woman coming in the main entrance to the building as I was leaving. I could be wrong, but I think he's got a girlfriend, and he was trying to get rid of me."

My eyes widened. "Woah, your dad! That's fantastic."

"For him maybe, but for me, it's all kinds of icky."

"Why? You should be glad. He deserves to be happy."

"I know that, and I want that for him. I just don't want to see it."

"Technically you didn't see anything."

She pointed at her temple. "No, but I know things, and I know there are things going on I don't need to see."

I laughed. "You crack me up."

"So, you got a date with the sexy sheriff?"

"No. He came by to give me some news."

"Oh, like he's ready to date, and you're his girl?"

"Like my long-lost uncle was found dead last night."

Her coy smile disappeared. "Oh, my gosh. I'm sorry, Ab."

"Thanks, but it's okay."

"What happened?"

"They think he was attacked by coyotes or something."

If I was right, it was more like *or something*.

She flinched. "Oh, wow. That's awful."

I explained the situation, detailing how I needed to see the coroner and decide how to handle both my aunt's and uncle's remains.

"What do you think you're going to do?"

"I don't have any idea."

Bessie stepped over. "I have a suggestion."

We looked up at her. Well, Stella looked up. Bessie was short, and I, sitting down, barely had to lift my eyes to meet hers.

"Please, I could use your input."

"I think you need to let them rest with their family."

That wasn't what I expected. "Really?"

She stated her case, and it made sense. Even though they'd been banned, they were family, and it was the Odell family tomb. Besides, she'd said, it was time to let go of the negativity of the family history, to move forward.

"But they didn't live here. They'd been banned. The cemetery rules state that only residents can live here."

"Yes, but it doesn't say they have to be residents at the time of their death. Just that they had to be residents. It's a little loophole. Everyone knows about it, but no one's tried to use it. I think it's time you do. No matter what happened, it's the right thing to do."

"I guess I'll think about it."

I watched as my best friend sat and worked on edits for a client's manuscript. Our relationship had changed, and she didn't even know it, probably wouldn't ever know it, either. There would be so many things I could never tell her, so many things I'd want to say, but couldn't. I worried her being associated with me would be dangerous, but with my uncle dead, I hoped everything was over, and I wouldn't be putting anyone I cared about in danger by simply existing.

While she whined about too much fluff and not enough guts for a historical fiction novel, I half listened and typed Esmerelda's adventures, trying hard to stop worrying about the gaping space of differences growing between us.

I worked an old man shapeshifter into the story, adding some red herrings to keep the readers guessing. I wasn't finished, but I did get a good eight thousand words in, which impressed me considering all I'd been going through and how distracted I'd been.

A few hours later, Stella packed up her things and left, saying she needed a good kickboxing class to work off the frustrations of the awful manuscript. Better her than me, I thought. Lord knows what would happen if I had to wipe sweat from my face.

Hey, I'd just given myself an excuse to avoid exercising. At least there was that.

Bessie handed me a bottle of water. "You need to get going to the coroners. You going to ask Gabe to come?"

My face reddened. "No. It feels weird to me to do that. We're practically strangers."

"Honey, that's the reason he asked you."

"Because we're practically strangers?"

She rolled her eyes. "He's trying to get to know you better, to spend time with you."

"You think?"

"I don't think, I know."

I sighed. "I'm not so sure. Besides, I've got a little too much going on to start any kind of romantic relationship."

"If you say so."

I closed up my laptop and sighed. "Do you think it's over?"

"I'm glad you're not accusing Merlock anymore, and yes, I think it's over. Samuel's dead."

"I didn't actually accuse Merlock, I just wondered. I didn't know he couldn't get my powers."

I stared at the entrance to the store, nodding as I thought things through. "You're right."

Her eyes widened. "I am? About what?"

"About burying my aunt and uncle's remains. I think it's the right thing to do. And, you're probably right about Merlock, too." My voice softened. "He's just a cranky old man." I didn't let on that his coming at me the night before still sat at the pit of my stomach, and I didn't have a good feeling about him, not at all.

Things might have been over with Samuel, but Merlock and I? We had unfinished business.

* * *

Atlanta traffic had nothing on the soccer mom traffic in Forsyth County. Taxiing multiple kids from one sport to the other jammed the streets with SUVs, crossovers, and minivans. A drive that should have taken thirty minutes lasted nearly fifty. I decided to take the back roads home hoping to escape soccer mom suburbia as fast as possible. Besides, the winding back roads in Forsyth County were prettier than the interstate. I connected my phone and listened to the *Cats* soundtrack, trying to distract myself from the events of the past few days. The coroner would handle transporting my aunt and uncle to the funeral home in Holiday Hills, where they'd be cremated. I called the funeral home from outside the coroner's office and explained to Mr. Remington there would be no services, and that I wanted them interned together with their names engraved into a small plaque.

I turned right onto Spot Road, slowing around each sharp curve. The late afternoon sun dipped beneath the hills as darkness quickly crept in. A dog ran out into the road. I screamed, and I slammed on my brakes. Cooper flew off the passenger seat and landed on the floor. I leaned back, stiff armed my steering wheel, and stared wide-eyed at the animal.

But it wasn't a dog. It was a wolf. Standing on two legs and glaring into my car, its mouth shaped into a tooth baring snarl. A wolf that looked just like Merlock Dupe.

"Holy crap!"

Cooper struggled to get back onto the seat. "What?"

I pointed to the animal as it fell back onto all fours and bolted toward me. "A…a…it's a wolf."

The wolf jumped onto the hood of my car, swinging its sharp nailed claws at my window as it growled and showed me its large, sharp teeth.

I took my foot off the brake, and the car jolted forward. The wolf dug its claws onto the edge of my hood.

"Oh boy," Cooper said. He pawed at the windshield as if that would do anything. "Tell it to go away."

I glanced at him, and then the wild, aggressive, and really angry monster standing on my hood. "I don't think it's going to listen."

Cooper huffed. "Magically, Abby. Magically."

I nodded. "Oh yeah. Right." I focused on the wolf. "Be gone, animal," I said.

The wolf froze, growled loudly, and then disappeared in a cloud of smoke.

I dropped my arms and took what felt like my first breath in minutes. I put the car in park and leaned against my seat. "Woah."

"Be gone, animal?"

The corner of my mouth twitched. "It was the first thing that came to mind."

"Well, at least it worked, because this wasn't a coincidence, Abby."

"Yeah, I know. Gabe was wrong. There are wolves in north Georgia." I shifted back into drive. "And they're gunning for me."

CHAPTER 7

I spent the rest of the night deep in research about shapeshifters, what they did, how dangerous they were, and their relationship with witches. Samuel may have been dead, his threat against me eliminated, but he wasn't the only one after me.

There was no mistaking the wolf was, and nothing could convince me it wasn't Merlock. I just didn't know why or what to do about it. I'd never been anything but nice to the man, even when his crotchety self wasn't nice to me. Aside from what Bessie mentioned, I'd never seen he and my mother argue either. But that didn't mean he wasn't harboring some inner resentment toward her and decided to take it out on me. He couldn't take my powers, but he could eliminate me. Anything or anyone could kill a witch.

If the witch didn't kill them first.

Cooper hopped onto the couch and pushed his muscular little body into my side. I picked him up and cuddled him close to my face, and he nuzzled his head into the crook of my neck. It wasn't weird or awkward, it was simply as it used to be. We'd spent many nights after Zach left just like that. Cooper had been a comforting and understanding friend then, and I didn't care if he spoke human. I just needed him to be him.

I was tired, worried, angry, resentful...if there was a negative emotion to feel, I felt it. I wanted my old life back. I rubbed my nose on the sleeve of my shirt, and every light in the house switched on. I groaned. "Turn off," I said, and the house went dark.

Cooper climbed off the couch and onto the coffee table between my laptop and the book my mother left me. "It's time."

I wiped my eyes. "Time for what?"

"To find out the truth about your mother."

"That's what I'm trying to do."

"No, I mean from the source. You need to go to the source, Ab."

I blinked. "There's really a source?"

He tilted his head. "Huh?"

"You know, the source. Like in *Charmed*?"

Cooper shook his head. "I've got a lot of work to do with you, don't I?" He pawed the book. "By the source, I mean Addie. You need to find out what happened from Addie."

"But you said that was dangerous."

"It is, but Bessie is experienced in this kind of thing. She can help you."

"You want me to ask Bessie to summon my mother." It wasn't a question but more like a statement in disbelief.

He nodded. "Call her. Trust me, she's been waiting for this."

I exhaled. "You're sure about this.?"

He hopped off the table, scurried to the dining table and jumped up there where my cell phone sat. He swiped it off the table. "I'm sure."

I crawled off the couch and picked up my phone. "You're lucky I have carpet. You could have cracked the screen." I hit my favorites and clicked on Bessie. It was late, and I hated disturbing her, especially because I knew she had to get up early, but I trusted Cooper knew what he was talking about.

"Abby, honey, is everything okay?"

I swallowed back the tears suddenly filling my eyes. "I miss my mom."

"Oh Abby. Sweetie, I know. I miss her, too."

"I'm sorry. I know it's late, but Cooper said it's time, and that you've been waiting, and you can help me. I have the book, but I don't know how to do this because I'm new to it all, and he said—"

She let me babble on another few minutes before she finally said, "Sit tight, sweetie. I'll be right over."

I ended the call, and Cooper stood on the table, staring at me. "Breathe."

I inhaled and exhaled slowly a few times. It helped a little. "I feel stupid."

"You shouldn't. Your mother was a wonderful woman. She gave me tuna all the time. I miss her, too."

Only Cooper could go there, and I couldn't help but smile.

A few minutes later, Bessie showed up and held me while I cried some more.

She wiped a mass of tear-soaked hair from my face. "I wondered when you'd release it all."

"I guess you don't have to wonder anymore."

I wiped my nose and Siri said, "I'm sorry, I didn't get that."

Bessie and I stared at the phone and broke out in laughter.

I sat back on the couch. "I guess Siri doesn't quite get magic."

"I'm sure technology will figure magic out one of these days."

I furrowed my brow. "That's disturbing."

She smiled. "It sure is." She sat next to me and laid her hand on the book. Surveying the room, she her hand glued in place.

I went to speak, but Cooper shushed me. "She's doing it," he whispered.

The temperature in my apartment dropped several degrees,

sending a chill throughout my body. I wrapped my arms around myself. Cooper jumped onto the arm of the couch and pressed his body against my side.

Bessie began to hum, first low and softly, then increasing as she lifted her hand slowly from the book. She muttered something I couldn't understand.

A misty cloud hovered on the other side of the table. I gasped and pushed my body hard into the back of the couch as the cloud formed into a translucent, three-dimensional upper half of a human.

My mother.

Tears poured from my eyes, and I bolted upright, my heart racing like it never had before. "Momma?"

Bessie held her free hand up, keeping her other hand levitating over the book. "Don't, sweetie."

I froze in place, afraid to move and break the spell. Literally.

Bessie spoke, her voice soft but commanding. "Adaline Odell, validate your presence."

The wavy, see-through version of my mother spoke, her voice hoarse and groggy. "Alubahrabame."

Huh?

Bessie repeated the word, and the cloudiness around my mother dissipated a bit. "Do you know what happened to you?"

I scooted very slowly to the edge of the couch. Cooper jumped onto my lap.

My mom's three-dimensional cloudy upper half brightened. "My soul is at peace."

I bit my lip. "Momma?"

Bessie held up her hand again. "Let me," she whispered.

"Adaline, was your death natural?"

The cloudy figure swayed back and forth, humming something similar to what Bessie had earlier, before saying, "My soul is at peace," again.

I sighed. I needed more. I needed to know what happened, I needed the truth.

The spirit form lit up my dim apartment like a sunny summer day. I squinted, trying hard to see my mom, but her glow overtook any slight form I'd seen before. The light illuminated even more until it suddenly burst into a mass of starlight sparkles, drifting up toward the ceiling and then fading away one by one.

I pressed my hands into the cushions and launched off the couch. "Momma, no, wait. Please!" I ran toward the fading mist and fell to my knees. "I need answers," I cried. I sat there for a moment, releasing the frustration through tears.

Cooper rubbed his body against me as Bessie helped me up.

"Honey, you got your answers. You just have to understand them." She guided me back to the couch and sat down next to me. "You're only given what you need to know, what matters most."

"Like what? That my mother is at peace?"

She nodded.

"But that doesn't tell me what happened to her. I need to know how she died and if Samuel took her powers." I reached for the book, heaving the heaviness of it and setting it between she and I. "Bring her back. Ask her about Samuel. Please."

Bessie set the book back on the table. "That's not how this works. Spirits aren't like you write in your stories. Once the soul leaves this world, bringing it back for a conversation isn't how you think it is. It's like deciphering a code and knowing that code is limited."

"I don't understand."

She exhaled. "Your mother can't just come back and chat like she's still here. The Universe only allows her to give you bits of information to help you heal. She told you she's at peace."

"But—"

"No, Abby. No buts. She's at peace, and that's what matters. How she passed or what happened with her powers doesn't matter. The universe is telling you to let go, to move on. What is will be."

I wiped my eyes and nose, and the book hovered off table, and then dropped back down with a thunk. I should have worried about that, but I didn't, and the book was fine anyway.

Bessie watched and smiled. "Even if Samuel did take your mother's powers, there's nothing you can do now. He's gone. It's time to let this go."

She didn't know about the wolf in the road. She didn't know my reservations about Merlock weren't resolved. To Bessie, things were done, and life went on, but I was still in the thick of it, no matter what the universe told me to do.

* * *

After Bessie left, I went to work. I had a plan, and to execute that plan, I needed to study Merlock's actions, to watch what he did, and where he went. If the man had it out for me, I needed to be one step ahead of him and prepared to fight.

And I was.

The next morning, I set up my worktable like the past few days hadn't happened. It was an act, and I struggled at first to follow through with the happy face and motivated to write attitude, but once I got in my groove, it came naturally.

Pretend there isn't a problem, and there isn't a problem.

Bessie let me be, and I wondered if she knew I was up to something. If she did, she wasn't letting on. I kept my eye on her, analyzing her moves to see if I could get a hook on her thoughts. When she finally asked me how I was holding up and said she was glad to see me moving forward, I knew she believed I was doing just that.

Good. That's what I wanted her to think. If she knew otherwise, she'd worry and try to stop me from doing what had to be done.

Peter Parallel arrived first that morning, which wasn't

unusual in the scope of their many days at The Enchanted. He ordered his coffee and smiled at me, greeting me with a hello.

I gave him a tooth filled, bordering on fake smile. "How are you?"

He pushed out his shoulders and crooked his neck. I heard the small popping sound it made from cracking. "A little tight this morning. Must be the cold. Takes the bones longer to wake up at my age."

"I get that. It was mighty comfy under the covers this morning, that's for sure. The cold is wearing on me, too."

Bessie gave him his coffee and he set a five-dollar bill on the counter. "Keep the change."

She nodded. "Don't mind if I do."

Peter headed toward his chair. Mr. Charming cooed when he patted him on the head. The cold temperatures turned the rain into a light flurry of the white stuff, and he watched it drop on the sidewalk outside.

I walked over and sat in an empty chair facing the window, watching the snowflakes fall and stick before disappearing. "It sure is pretty when it snows."

"Em hmm. Don't see that much around here, do we?"

"I wish we had a little more of it. Not so much that the stores run out of milk and bread, but enough to make it pretty."

"Stores run out of milk and bread when it snows even a little like this."

I chuckled. "You're right."

Stella showed up and sat in Merlock's seat while Bessie prepared her coffee. She'd dressed in full out winter gear: a pink beanie, pink gloves, and matching scarf, all matching her puffy pink ski jacket. "Brr, it's cold out there."

I poked at her puffy arm. "We're not in Canada, you know."

She removed her gloves and then pulled the hat off her head, and her hair stood up like she'd just stuck her finger in an electrical socket. She must have felt the static electricity because she licked her palm and rubbed it on her hair. It didn't help.

"My car wouldn't start so I had to walk here." She took off her jacket and wrapped it around the back of her chair. "You try walking in that."

"I did. From upstairs."

"Yeah, and you were outside all of two seconds. You're so brave, roughing it like that."

I said, "Eh. I'm tough like that."

Peter laughed, and Stella narrowed her eyes at him.

He flinched and said, "She's right. It's cold."

The door opened, and Merlock charged in, his energy hot and intense. Stella turned around and her eyes widened as Mr. Charming said, "Addie's here. Addie's here."

Stella's shoulders sunk and she swiveled her head toward me. "I'm getting to work."

I raised an eyebrow. "Okay."

Merlock took off his coat and tossed it on his chair, swiping Mr. Charming with it in the process. Mr. Charming flapped his wings and readjusted himself back on the chair.

Peter shook his head. "Be mindful of the bird, old man."

Merlock groaned. "That bird ought to be mindful of me." He glared at me. "Don't see why you're keeping it anyway. 'You need it taken care of, I'll shoot it for you. Don't matter to me."

Bessie rushed over and swatted Merlock on the arm. "You stop that awful talk, Merlock."

He grimaced. "Just speaking truth. The bird is old, and its momma is dead. Time for it to move on. Should have gone with her anyway."

My blood pressure kicked up a notch. Was he baiting me? Did he want to get into an argument? I pivoted to check on Stella and caught her looking away when I did.

"Merlock Dupe. You apologize to Mr. Charming and Abby or

I'm going to kick you right out into that cold again. Don't you think I won't do it either."

He yanked the coffee cup from Bessie and coffee splashed out of it.

"Now look what you've done," she said, wiping the coffee from her sweater. She flung her hand toward the door. "Don't push me old man."

Merlock sat in his chair and sipped his coffee. "Who you calling an old man? You're older than me, woman."

"Merlock," I said with a soft, concerned, and completely fake tone. "Are you okay? You don't seem like yourself today."

He growled. "You best be leaving me alone, Abby."

My eyes widened. I turned around and stared at Stella. She watched the events as they played out. I knew if I did something, the odds were that she wouldn't see, but I didn't know what she would see, and I wasn't sure how to handle what happened after. Would she have something to say? Would I have to scramble to figure out what the universe showed her over what I knew happened?

When Peter told Merlock to stay calm, Merlock stood and puffed out his chest. I caught the yellow glow in his eyes and panicked. "Oh, no. No, no, no." I shook my head quickly, and the man disappeared.

Literally, he disappeared. No poof of air, no cloudy mist, no mini tornado, just flat out disappeared.

"Nice work," Peter said.

I whipped around to check on Stella, who just smiled and said, "Thank God he left."

I had no idea what she saw, but at least she hadn't run screaming.

She walked back over and pet Mr. Charming. "The mean man is gone, sweetie pie." She rubbed his little forehead. "Let's hope he doesn't come back. Ever."

Stella wasn't exactly a fan of Merlock, but she'd never said anything like that. "Wow."

She sat in Merlock's chair, and Mr. Charming perched on her shoulder.

"I don't care if I ever see that man again."

"Really? Why?"

She sipped her coffee. "I ordered pizza last night, and of course my car wouldn't start then either, so I had to walk there." She glanced outside. "I'm going to have to get it jumped or something."

"You were saying?"

"I ran into him, and we chatted. At first it was nothing. You know, regular stuff about the cold, that kind of thing. Then he starting asking me all these weird questions about you and your mom. Personal questions. I tried to change the subject, but he just kept going. I finally had to tell him I didn't feel comfortable sharing your personal information, and that's when he got all angry. I mean, I know he's cranky, but this was different. He was mad, like, seriously ticked off. I asked him what the big deal was, and he said…" She shook her head. "I don't know exactly. Something about how I didn't understand. You and Addie aren't good people, and you need to be handled. Then I got mad, and I told him where he could shove it."

Peter had propped the newspaper up in front of his face, but he dropped one side down to listen.

"What kinds of questions?"

"Things about what you two do at home. I don't know. Weird stuff. And he kept asking about a book. Wanted to know if you'd shown me it, if I knew where it was. I told him you have a lot of books, but he said I knew what he was talking about, and I'd pay if I didn't tell him."

"That's odd," Peter said.

"Right? That's about when I told him to shove it."

"Then what happened?" I asked.

She shrugged. "He just did that growly thing he does, and I walked into the pizza place, and he left."

I didn't want to press too much because I wouldn't normally. "I'm sorry. He's definitely weird."

"If I were you, I'd stay clear of him for a while. Looks like he's got something going on, and with that temper of his, you never know what he'll do," Peter said.

"That's exactly why I hope he never comes back," Stella said. "Anyway, time to get to work. This manuscript is going to be the death of me."

Having a best friend that was also an editor had its benefits, but I tried not to bug her when she was knee deep in another book.

A little while later, I meandered as casually as I could back to Peter. "Hey, can we talk later? Away from here?"

He raised an eyebrow. "Everything okay?"

"Yes, I just wanted to talk about my, uh…about something. It's important."

"Sure. I'm heading out in a bit. Got some doctor appointments in Cumming, if I can get down the mountain with the snow. I can come by your place at say about six o'clock?"

"That would be great. Thank you."

Stella complained about her client's manuscript, periodically reading me passages from it. "What does that even mean? Double negatives aside, the sentence doesn't make any sense."

"Are you copy editing it or doing a developmental edit?"

She rolled her eyes. "Developmental, but it's hard to do that when it's just so poorly written."

I chuckled. "You're good at what you do. Just do what you tell me. Focus on the story. If it doesn't work, guide the author on how to fix it."

I got another eye roll. "It's ninety thousand words and it's filled with errors, not to mention story holes the size of Europe.

It's going to be the death of me." She sighed. "I'm sorry, I didn't mean—"

I smiled. "It's okay. It's just an expression."

"A poorly timed one."

I tapped my toe against her leg. "I know you love me."

"A lot more than I love this manuscript, that's for sure. I really can't wait for this whole dystopian trend to end. I'd even edit that reverse harem stuff over this."

Stella hated editing books in genres she didn't like. I knew that one was driving her crazy. Dystopian worlds were her least favorite reads, but that book was really awful if she was willing to edit a reverse harem book. She despised those more than anything.

* * *

Peter buzzed the bell downstairs. I thought I'd left the main door unlocked, but I hadn't. I'd hidden the book under my bed because I wasn't sure it was something he should see.

He sat in the chair across from the couch. His posture showed me he was uncomfortable, but the cup of tea I'd made seemed to ease that a bit.

"Nice place you've got here." He examined my small apartment, noting the closed door to my bedroom.

Was he wondering why the door was closed, or maybe he wanted to see my comfy bed? I brushed those thoughts from my brain. He wasn't interested in me that way.

"Thought it would be smaller, though I don't know why I'd think that."

"You know, I kind of thought that, too, before I saw the place. I guess it's because we don't see the back room area of The Enchanted, so it seems kind of small."

"Could be."

"Thank you for coming by. I wanted to talk to you about the argument between my mother and Merlock."

His shoulders stiffened. "You don't need to be dredging up that mess, Abby. Best to leave well enough alone."

I ignored his suggestion to leave well enough alone. "I was hoping you could tell me what happened."

Mr. Charming acted odd, flapping his feathers and squawking repeatedly.

"Mr. Charming, hush."

He flew over to Peter and landed on the back of the chair. "Addie's here. Addie's here."

Peter shooed him away.

"I'm sorry about that. He misses my mom."

"No problem. She was a good woman, and they were together a long time."

Mr. Charming flew laps around the room, continuing his squawk concert. I tried to quiet him, but he wouldn't listen. Cooper sensed something was off with the bird, too, though I couldn't see how he wouldn't. He'd been snoozing on the couch, but he stood and stretched, then wandered over to me and shoved his weighty body against my side.

"What could my mother and Merlock possibly argue about?"

"Do you know what Merlock is?"

"You mean his magical self? Yes, he's a shapeshifter, right?"

He nodded. "A powerful one at that. He likes to turn at night and hunt. Usually he doesn't cause any trouble, but one night when your mom was at the cemetery, he appeared in wolf form and taunted her, chased her around, and nearly attacked her. It wasn't right. Wasn't normal, not with how things work here in town."

"Is he the only shifter?"

"We've got a few eagles and one meaner than the dickens owl, but Merlock's the only wolf."

"So, my mom knew it was him."

He nodded. "Told the council it was, but he denied it. Claimed he hadn't gone out that night, swore up and down it was some warlock or witch posing as him just to get him in trouble."

"They—we can do that?"

He nodded. "Powerful magicals can do just about anything if they get the spell right."

"But why? Why would someone pose as Merlock in wolf form and taunt my mother like that?"

He shrugged. "She wasn't sure why he would do it, let alone someone else. Best we could come up with was that it had something to do with her siblings."

"Samuel and Allegra?"

"Yup. There were rumors that Allegra was in love with someone in town, and when she was banned, she was separated from the one she loved. People thought it made that person angry, and if that person was a magical, they could have blamed your mother."

"And you think that person was Merlock?"

He laughed. "I'm pretty sure Merlock is too ornery for anyone to love, but I guess anything's possible. After all, we live in a magical world. For all I know, he could have loved your mother. It's not like he ever tells me anything."

I sighed. "I can't imagine my mother would have loved someone like Merlock. She was too bright and cheerful for the likes of him."

"Could be one of those unrequited loves. Poor guy. Love just wasn't in the cards, no matter who it was, but still, that ain't no reason to go after your mom like that."

I spoke to Peter but was really talking through my thoughts. "I don't remember him ever acting like he had feelings for my mom. They were friendly, but really, more like acquaintances than anything. But if he loved Allegra that would explain why he'd gone after my mom." I scooted Cooper over and tucked my foot under my leg. "Did other's blame my mom for what happened to Samuel and Allegra?"

He shrugged. "A few, but as time went by, people forgot. They moved on to the next tasty piece of gossip and then the next… you get it."

"Yeah, I do. Gossip is popular in towns like ours."

"It's big everywhere, but just more obvious in a town like Holiday Hills."

"Can you keep a secret?"

He leaned forward, the awkwardness surrounding him before completely gone. "I've been keeping secrets most of my life. Big ones, at that."

"There's a wolf after me. At first, I thought it was Samuel, but Gabe, I mean, Chief Ryder told me they found him dead in the woods. Said he'd been attacked by coyotes. I'm thinking it was Merlock that attacked him. And now that I think about it, I get the reason. If Merlock did love Allegra, maybe he believed Samuel convinced Allegra to be a part of it. Maybe he blamed Samuel for Allegra's being banned from town?"

"Wait, what do you mean there's a wolf after you?"

I told Peter everything. As I did, Mr. Charming continued his squawking, still flying laps around the room and repeating, "Addie's here. Addie's here." I shushed him several times, finally locking him in my bedroom where he pecked at the door and kept at it until Peter left.

When Peter did leave, he left me with a stern warning to stay away from Merlock.

The exact opposite of what I planned.

CHAPTER 8

$\mathcal{M}$y phone's alarm buzzed at midnight. I threw on a pair of black yoga pants, a long-sleeved black t-shirt with a Harley Davidson logo on it—one of the few things I'd taken from Zach–slipped a black beanie over my head, and pulled on my black boots.

The prey was ready to hunt the hunter.

Cooper wasn't at all thrilled, but I made it clear he didn't have a say in the matter.

"If Merlock is coming for me, I have to get to him first. And Cooper, it's got to be him. You know it as much as I do. It's some kind of weird revenge."

I snuck out the door and headed down the stairs, making sure Mr. Charming stayed inside. I'd told him this wasn't his place, and I needed him to guard the house. Whether he understood, I wasn't sure, but he didn't squawk his displeasure.

Cooper followed me as I cut through yards to get to Merlock's house. I prayed Gabe wasn't out driving around again, but I kept low to the ground just in case. Catching me outside once was bad enough, but twice would raise his suspicions, and I didn't have time for that.

Every house on the small street was dark. Even the street-lights were off, which I took to mean they'd blown out and hadn't been replaced. I used the dim flashlight on my phone to help me see but kept it off as much as possible.

I crept up to the back of Merlock's house and peeked in a window. The shuttered blind was down, but I could see through the cracks. The house was still, and if Merlock was home, he certainly wasn't in the kitchen. I plodded over to another window on the far side, which, if I knew the design of the house, should be his bedroom. The window was blocked completely by a shade instead of blinds, and I couldn't see a thing.

"Darn it."

"What'd you think you'd find, Merlock checking off a list titled *things to do to destroy Abby* or something?"

I scooped him up and hurried to a brush of bushes in the back corner of the lot. "What're you trying to do, wake him up?"

"What're you trying to do? Get busted for being a peeping Tom?"

"It's creepy how you know human things sometimes."

"There's a story there, but it's for another time."

I wasn't sure I wanted to know.

We stood there, me holding him, and him wiggling to free himself from my grip.

"Can you put me down, please? I'm feeling a little nauseous."

I blanched, setting him down quickly. Cat throw up was the last thing I needed at that moment.

"Thanks."

"You okay?"

"Yeah. Just wanted to be on all fours."

I blinked. "So you lied?"

"Meh, magicals hate cat puke as much as humans. I did what I had to do."

I rolled my eyes assuming he wouldn't notice in the dark.

"Cats have excellent night vision, you know."

"Whoops."

"So, what's next? We get comfy and wait?"

"Yup."

"For what?"

"For him to leave. He was really angry today. What's the best way for a shifter to release their aggression?"

"Depends on what the shifter shifts to. Oh, say that fast, and you'll sound like Stella."

"You're sassy tonight."

"I'm a cat."

"True. Anyway, he's going hunting. I'm sure of it."

"I hate to admit it, but you're probably right. Whatever irked him, he's going to need to let it out, if he hasn't already."

"He hasn't. His anger has to do with the Odell family, so he's coming for me tonight. I can feel it."

"Yeah, I feel something, too. Not sure if it's from the tuna or what, but I feel something."

I rolled my eyes again.

"Saw that, too."

"Cooper, please. This is serious."

"Yeah, yeah. I know. I can't help it. Sometimes when I feel tense, I crack bad jokes. I get a little snarky. I've always been this way. It's just who I am."

I exhaled. "We have to be quiet. I don't want him to know I'm here."

He whispered, "He can't hear me."

"Oh, right."

"Did you bring the pepper spray stuff?"

I held out my hand. "Yup."

"Waste of the extra hand."

"Whatever."

A light in what I thought was the bedroom went on.

"Look! He's awake."

Cooper slunk toward the house, his body lower to the ground

than normal. I scurried to a big tree and hid behind it, watching my cat inch closer to the house. The light stayed on, but I heard movement toward the back patio, something banging around the house.

As I moved for the next tree, a large gray wolf charged past, slowing near me and lifting its nose for to sniff. It stopped.

Cooper ran over and rubbed his body against my leg, propping himself up on his hind legs and hissing at the big animal.

The wolf growled.

I stayed there, motionless. I didn't want to make him disappear, not temporarily. First, I wanted answers, and then if I had to, I'd eliminate him for good. "Why are you after me?"

He growled again. "Leave me alone," he said, and then he bolted off through the trees.

I stared into the darkness, flabbergasted.

Cooper dropped to all fours. "What the heck was that?"

I shook my head slowly. "I have no idea."

"Where do you think he's going?"

"More importantly, why didn't he do anything to me?"

"Your guess is as good as mine."

I adjusted the beanie so it covered my ears and acted like I was completely fine, even though my entire body trembled. "It's freezing out here."

"You think? I'm barefoot."

"You're a cat. You're supposed to be used to the elements."

"Barefoot in the snow is still barefoot in the snow."

I picked him up and carried him back as I hurried back home, thinking about how to corner Merlock and get the answers I needed.

* * *

"I don't like this," Cooper said.

I set him down and we both stared at the door to my building hanging from the frame and bent almost in half.

"We gotta get outta here," he said.

"No. Mr. Charming's up there. What if something's happened to him?" I tugged the beanie off my head and yanked the gloves from my hands. "I'm done with this. It's time to settle things once and for all." I didn't know how I'd become so brave. It had to be fear and stupidity taking over, along with a pinch of desperation and adrenaline.

"Ab, this doesn't feel good."

"It doesn't to me either, but we've got this." I stepped inside. "Come on."

He rushed through the door and up the stairs. I followed behind.

My door was open, too, the wood bashed in just above the knob. Cooper hissed as he propped himself on all fours. I took a deep breath and charged in, flipping on the light and exposing Merlock in wolf form by my couch.

Good. Time to settle things once and for all.

He growled.

I sneered. "No. This ends now."

He growled again, standing up on his hind legs and whipping a claw at me.

I tensed every muscle in my body, so much so a sharp pain shot through my jaw. "What do you want from me, Merlock?"

He growled again, and his body shifted to his human form.

I stared at the naked man with determination, not averting my eyes, but definitely not looking below his neck. "I haven't done anything to you."

My laptop hovered off the table and flung into the back of the couch.

Had I done that?

Cooper positioned himself in front of me. "Oh, boy."

Merlock snarled, and when he spoke, his voice was raspy but intimidating, powerful even. "Leave me alone. I'm not going to warn you again." He raised his arms and growled, turning back into wolf form.

"Oh, boy," Cooper said again.

Merlock dropped to all fours and raced out of my apartment and down the stairs.

Cooper and I stood there, speechless.

I shook my head, trying hard to make sense out of what had happened. Mr. Charming shivered and picked at his feathers inside his cage. He went there when something stressed him out. I held out my arm and he flew to me.

"It's okay, Mr. Charming. It's over now."

"Sing the happy song. Sing the happy song."

Cooper hopped onto the couch and got comfy.

"Okay sweetie, let's sing the happy song." I hummed *Heartache Tonight* by the Eagles, another one of my mother's favorite songs.

Cooper groaned as Mr. Charming sang the lyrics, loudly. He flapped his wings and took flight from my arm, chirping the tune as he flew around the room. I sat on the couch, exhausted, afraid, determined, filled with too many emotions to identify.

Cooper sat on his bottom. "We need to discuss this, Abby."

"I know."

* * *

The next morning Peter showed up to The Enchanted before me, and was already reading the daily paper when I walked in. Merlock was there, too, and he acted as though nothing happened, as if he hadn't threatened me, hadn't practically ripped the door off my building. He'd turned back into his relatively normal, cranky self.

"You always got to bring that bird with you? He picks at my head."

Cooper hissed.

Mr. Charming hopped off my shoulder and onto the back of Merlock's chair. "Addie's here."

"If it's going to talk, can't you at least keep it on your side of the store?"

Bessie lectured Merlock on proper manners, but he ignored her.

Mr. Charming flew toward Peter and stood in front of him on the table. He stared at the man, bending his head to the left and then the right. "Addie's here." He hopped across the table and back onto Merlock's chair.

I eyed Peter, who shook his newspaper and said, "We all miss her buddy."

"I've got another new blend to try," Bessie said. "You up for it?" Her eyes trailed up and down my body. "Where's your bag?"

"Oh, I'm not working today. Not yet anyway. I have some things to take care of this morning."

She smiled and held up a pot. "Regular?"

"Yes, please. To go."

"Good to see you working through things, honey."

I glanced at Cooper near my legs. His eyes were set on the two men.

Merlock stood and Mr. Charming flew to the counter.

"I got stuff to do today, too," Merlock said. "Can't be wasting my days sitting here."

Peter dipped a corner of the paper. "Should I be offended?"

"Don't care what you are," he said. He tossed a hand up in the air and headed toward the door.

"Don't let it hit you on the way out," Peter hollered. "On second thought, let it."

Bessie shamed Peter with a, "That's not nice."

I paid for my coffee, something Bessie rarely let me do, by tossing a ten-dollar bill onto the counter, and rushed toward the door before she could argue. "I'll be back for Mr. Charming," I said as the door closed behind me.

Cooper caught up. "Where we going?"

Merlock wasn't far ahead of us. "Shh, we're following him."

"Why? He told you to leave him alone."

"So?"

"So. Probably best you do that."

"I'm not afraid of an old man."

"He's not just an old man."

Gabe Ryder pulled up in his police cruiser.

Cooper stopped. "That's it. We're going to jail."

"For what, jaywalking?"

"You think they have tuna in jail?"

"Cooper, we aren't going to jail."

Gabe stepped out of his car and positioned his hat on his head.

My stomach fluttered. "Stop that."

He raised an eyebrow. "I'm sorry?"

"Uh, hi. I said hi." I shifted my weight from one foot to the other, watching Merlock scurry around a corner and out of sight.

Gabe sauntered over in that sexy, slinky way he had and smiled. "You get your coffee to go this morning?"

I nodded. "I've got an appointment in uh, Cumming." I looked past him, wondering where Merlock was headed. He'd gone toward the cemetery, not his house.

Gabe turned around and checked behind him. "Something catch your eye?"

"What?" I hesitated. "Oh, no. Sorry. I was just in stare mode I guess."

He nodded. "Well." He tipped his hat. "You have a good day, Abby."

"You too, Chief."

I waited until the door to The Enchanted closed behind him and then I sprinted to the corner.

"Dang it!"

Cooper ran a bit further, came back, and panted. "I can't see him anywhere. Can't smell him either."

"It's okay. I know what to do." I darted around the corner and walked the few hundred feet behind the building to my apartment entrance. I'd fixed the door magically the night before, and in the clear morning light, I couldn't even tell anything happened.

I stripped off my coat and tossed it on the dining table. Once I sat on the couch and calmed my breathing, I said, "Map and crystal," rubbing beneath my nose just in case.

The map and crystal appeared on my coffee table.

"Nice," Cooper said.

"Thanks." I opened the map which was a challenge in and of itself. It took me a solid minute to unfold the thing, reminding me of the complicated origami crafts I did as a kid. "Geez, this is seriously ridiculous." Finally getting it open, I flattened it on the table and held the crystal dangling above it.

I took another deep breath, releasing it slowly. "Find Merlock."

The crystal didn't budge.

I repeated it, adding a please to the end for good measure.

The crystal still didn't budge.

"Why isn't it moving?"

Cooper hopped onto the table and stood on the map. "The crystal only shows you what you need to see."

"Come on. What's the point of all this magic if it's so limited?"

"Imagine what it would be like if there weren't boundaries."

I bit my lip. "You have a point. But I need to find Merlock."

"Try asking something else."

"Like what?"

"I don't know, like find the wolf or something."

The crystal swung, and Cooper jumped back onto the couch. "Woah. I've never done that before."

It swung again, moving my hand to the left and landing its point directly on the town cemetery.

"Something's not right, Ab."

"What do you mean? He's at the cemetery. The crystal said."

He shook his head. "I don't know. I don't feel good about this. You should call Bessie. Have her come up and help."

"No. I'm not doing that. She thinks I've let this all go, and besides, I don't want to put her in danger."

"But you'll put yourself in danger."

"Allegra said my powers are strong. I can handle a wolf."

"You're a newbie. What if you can't?"

"I have you for back up."

"I was afraid you'd say that."

I grabbed my coat and headed to my car.

"Maybe I should have a can of tuna first? You know, for muscle. It's protein, right?" He barely made it in before I slammed the door shut. "You almost caught my tail in the door."

"Sorry. Guess you need to step up the pace." I started the ignition and headed toward the cemetery.

"I really don't have a good feeling about this."

"You've made that clear."

"Not clear enough."

I pulled into the cemetery. "Where do you think he is?"

Cooper climbed onto the dashboard and stared outside. "I really don't want to say."

"Cooper."

"Well, if this is about you, then he's probably at the Odell tomb, right?"

"Right. Why didn't I think of that?" I stepped on the gas and zipped around the curves of the cemetery road, pulled up to the family tomb and slipped the car into park.

"Because you're a newbie, remember? I'll say it again, I—"

"I know. You don't feel good about this."

I'd tossed my coat in the backseat when leaving my apartment and left it there. I jumped out of the car, not bothering to close the door.

"Show yourself, wolf," I yelled. I took off toward the front corner of the tomb and walked into the covered area. "Let's end this now." I stood and waited, but nothing happened.

Cooper flipped around and headed in the opposite direction. "Well, looks like we're wrong."

A loud snarling growl stopped him in his tracks.

I froze.

Another growl, and then the rush of sounds I knew was a wolf preparing to attack. He screeched and roared, and then a shot rang out, and everything went silent.

I stared at Cooper.

"Crap," he said, and took off toward the sound.

"Cooper, no!" I screamed, racing after him.

On the ground around the corner lay a gray wolf, blood pooled underneath his furry body. "Oh, no," I said, rushing toward Merlock's wolf form. I hadn't wanted him dead really. I just wanted him to stop coming after me.

"Ab, no." Cooper shoved himself between my feet, and I had to stop or I'd fall. "Don't."

My eyes traveled from my cat to the legs and feet on the opposite side of Merlock. My mouth dropped. "Peter?"

Peter Parallel held a gun in one hand as he stared at the dead wolf. His eyes widened as he lifted them to mine. "Abby, I…I had to. He was coming after you."

I held out my hands. "Peter, put the gun down, okay?"

He kept his eyes focused on me "I…I'm…I had to."

"I know, Peter. It's okay. Just please, put the gun down."

A slow smile crept across his face, and I stood, frozen in disbelief as his body morphed into a dead man, into my Uncle Samuel.

"What's happening?"

"What do you think?" he asked.

Cooper stood on his hind legs and hissed.

"No, you're…you're dead."

Samuel laughed. "Remember what I said about strong

warlocks turning into something else?"

"That...that was you?"

He snarled, a creepy, dead evil burning like flames from his eyes. "In the flesh."

"But, you...your powers..." I couldn't get the words out. My heart raced, and my entire body dripped nervous sweat. "You don't have—you did it, didn't you? You got my mother's powers."

He pointed the gun directly at my head. "In a matter of speaking, yes."

"You have her powers, isn't that enough? Can't you just leave me alone?"

He laughed. "Leave you alone? Are you kidding? You're the bane of my existence. It's been my life's goal to terminate you."

His flat, unemotional voice scared me.

Cooper hissed again, and Samuel laughed.

I clasped my hands into fists and beat the sides of my legs. "You framed Merlock, didn't you?"

He laughed. "You poor little half breed, you aren't smart enough to understand." He transformed into Peter once again.

Cooper hissed again and charged at him, digging his claws into the warlock's pants. Peter kicked his leg, and Cooper went flying, crashing into the marble tomb.

I screamed. "Cooper!" I rushed to him, his motionless body lying on the ground. I narrowed my eyes at Samuel. "Be gone!" I screamed.

He just laughed. "You think that's going to work on me? Your power is nothing compared to mine. This was fun at first, playing with you, torturing you, fooling the stupid little twits of Holiday Hills, but I'm done. You're boring me now."

I'd left my phone and my pepper spray in my coat pocket. Not that either would help, but I hoped my magic would.

"Up." He whipped the gun toward me. "Against that wall over there. Now."

"Why are you doing this?"

He sneered. "You really don't know, do you?"

What was happening? Who was he, really? I flattened myself against the cold marble. My sweat connecting with the cold surface sent chills down my spine. "No, I don't. Why don't you explain it to me?" I needed to keep him talking, to give myself time to figure out what to do. I quickly glanced at Cooper, whose leg twitched. Thank God. At least he was alive.

"If your mother hadn't stuck her nose in our business, this would have never happened." Allegra and I, we could have been together, lived happily even, but no. She had to intervene."

"I...I don't understand."

He morphed back into my dead uncle. "Who am I, Abby?"

I shook my head. "I don't know." Tears streamed down my cheeks. "I don't understand what's happening."

He laughed as his body switched again to Peter. "I'm just a warlock, one that loved a woman and never stopped."

It all made sense then. "You're Peter. It was you that loved Allegra, not Merlock."

He waved the gun in the air in front of him. "But your mother, she didn't think I was good enough. She pressured Allegra to end our relationship, said she'd go public with it, and insisted her father would put an end to it."

I didn't understand. Why would my mother do that? What did it matter to her? I rubbed my nose and concentrated hard on Peter. "I command you to disappear!"

He didn't budge. "It doesn't work that way, witch." He stepped closer, keeping the gun pointed straight at me. "Would you like to hear the rest of the story, or should I just kill you now?"

I narrowed my eyes, wishing him away with every ounce of my being only to see him still there, the gun still pointed at my head, and Cooper barely moving nearby.

"Allegra had a plan. We would kill your mother and keep our secret until the time was right. Until your grandfather approved of me."

"You became Samuel and came after my mother."

He snarled. "But your stupid father, he had to get in the way. Allegra stopped me then. I could have taken your mother, too, but Allegra got scared, weak, and Addie made us disappear, at least temporarily."

"And then my grandfather found out, but he thought it was my uncle, and removed their powers, banned them from Holiday Hills."

He nodded. "All for naught. Allegra had a change of heart. She wanted nothing to do with me, even though I begged for forgiveness, she wouldn't. She couldn't. I'd changed, she said."

"She was here to warn me about you, wasn't she?"

He laughed. "Such a shame, the wasted power. When I realized she'd been with your mother as she died, I knew she'd taken your mother's powers so she could protect you. I had to kill her. Believe me," he wiggled the gun in his hand. "It wasn't what I wanted, but what was I supposed to do? I couldn't let her refuse me again. She didn't deserve me, and that's what I told her when I shot her."

I stiffened, internally begging the universe to help me since my magic wasn't.

Peter stepped closer, standing only inches from me, the gun alternating between my chest and my forehead. "Now all I have to do is kill you, suck your powers into my soul, and along with your mother's powers, I'll be even stronger. I'll be the strongest warlock ever."

I tried to stall him, tried to keep him talking. I had to figure something out. Cooper had to wake up, maybe he could help. "What about Merlock?" I moved my hand slowly and pointed behind him at the body.

Peter didn't budge. "A necessary if not unfortunate part of my plan. I needed him to be the fall guy, to take the blame once you're dead. So, I posed as him. Made you think he was after you, got you talking about it to Bessie, even got that human Stella upset with him. Who'll question his coming for you with that temper of his? Here's how I see it. You did something to upset him, and you both shot each other. Everyone in town knows he's a loose cannon. And you? You just lost your momma, you ain't right in the head now either."

"No one will believe that."

"Don't really care what they believe. It's not like that little police chief you got your eye on will figure it out. He's not magical, he can't step into our world."

Cooper's legs stretched out and he popped up from the ground. He charged toward Peter, pouncing up and digging his claws into the sides of his neck. Peter screamed as he struggled with one hand to free his neck from Cooper's death grip. The gun waved back and forth, and I ducked and ran behind them, away from the gun.

Peter whipped around and Cooper went flying again, smashing one more time into the marble tomb.

"Stop doing that," I screamed. "That's my familiar!" I stepped toward Peter, my arms out in front of me. "You're done, Peter!" A white light flashed through the narrow hall of the tomb. It settled behind me, and I felt a rush of adrenaline surge through my blood. "It's over!" I slammed my hands toward him as I stepped closer. "Leave this world, now!" The words came out of my mouth without a thought to them.

Peter twisted and turned, his body clouding over and softening into almost liquid form. "No!" His scream quickly muffled as his body dissolved into a mass of gooey liquid before shaping back into lifeless human remains.

I stood there, shocked and afraid. The flash of light hovered in front of me, barely shaping itself into something human, and disappeared.

Cooper meowed. I rushed to him and picked him up, kissing his face as he shook his head. "Cooper, are you okay?"

He meowed again. "Enough with the kisses. I've got an awful

headache." His eyes widened. "Wait, you okay? What about Samuel?"

"Actually, it was really Peter."

He hissed. "I knew I didn't like that guy."

I slid down the marble resting places of my ancestors and held him close. "Seriously? You never once acted like that."

"I like to keep you guessing."

I held him to my chest and let out a long, slow, relieving breath. "I thought you were dead."

"It's possible, but not probable."

I stared at Merlock, and next to him, the body of Peter slowly appeared, a pool of blood spreading beneath him. "What's happening?"

"That's called your cover." He crawled out of my grip and sniffed their bodies. "That's my guess, anyway."

"What happens next?"

"In the magical world or the human one?"

"The human one." I couldn't handle more than one world at that moment.

"The police will come, discover the men, and the case will close."

"But how?"

"The universe will give them an explanation they'll understand. It's not important now, but when you need to know, you'll just know."

"I feel bad that Merlock had to die."

"Yeah, me, too. He was a grouch, but generally a good guy, I guess."

"He threatened me. Why?"

"Wolves have a keen sense for danger. He probably knew you were watching him, and he didn't like it."

"You think that's all?"

"I do."

I kept him tight in my arms as I headed back to my car.

"I'm starving. Think you can pick up a can of tuna on the way home?"

* * *

Bessie's mouth hung open as she eyed the two empty chairs in the front of the store. "I can't believe it. I just can't believe it."

"Believe me, I can't either."

"Peter and Allegra. Your mother never said a thing."

"That's the part that doesn't make sense to me. If she didn't like Peter, why didn't I know?"

"Your mother did like Peter."

"But she didn't want him with her sister."

"She always said Peter could have done more with his life. She felt he didn't have the motivation to do much. He didn't even use his powers much. It struck everyone as odd, but we wrote it off to his personality."

"I guess she wanted someone to do right by her sister then?"

She nodded. "Guess so." She poured herself another cup of coffee. "It's like one of those soap operas. Man falls in love, family hates him, man kills someone in the family, then the woman feels awful, and she tries to protect the rest of the family but ends up dead because of it."

"Minus the witchy stuff."

She winked. "Of course."

"Do you think Allegra knew my mom was sick?"

"Seems like she did."

"I feel like she did, too. Like maybe she sensed it or something and came to protect her so Peter couldn't get her powers."

"I think she was protecting her from Samuel."

"You do?"

"If your aunt sensed your mother's weakening, then he probably did too. Remember, he was banned for something he didn't do. He must have hated your mother for that. He knew he could get her powers if she died with him there. I got a feeling he got there too late, and I think he would have killed Allegra for them if Peter hadn't beat him to it."

"And Peter killed Samuel." In wolf form, in case he needed to frame Merlock for it. That's the only theory that made sense.

She nodded. "He was a threat."

I ran my hand through my hair. "Wow. I can't even believe this is my life now."

She patted my free hand. "Abby, the magical world is full of miracles and wonder, but you must remember, everything happens for a reason, and not everyone gets a happy ending."

"Just like the human world."

"Just like the human world."

The door opened and Gabe Ryder removed his hat as he entered, closing the door behind him.

Bessie winked at me as she stepped over to the counter. "Happy endings," she whispered.

Gabe sauntered over as an Olympic gymnast performed her routine in my stomach. "Ladies."

I blushed. "Chief."

"I've got some sad news, and I wanted to share it with you before it got around."

I pretended to not know as he explained how the cemetery groundskeeper found Merlock and Peter, and how they'd had some kind of disagreement that ended in them both shooting each other. He said it was rare, but things like that happened.

I cried real tears for the men. No matter what happened, what Peter intended, he didn't deserve not being with the woman he loved, and I wished there was a way for magic to change it for him. But magic didn't work that way.

Gabe sat next to me and wrapped his arm around my shoulders. "It's been rough for you, I know. But Abby. I promise you, everything will be okay."

I leaned my head onto him, knowing he meant exactly what he said.

CHAPTER 9

*E*smerelda *stepped back onto the platform at the train station and waved as her sister's train worked its way down the tracks. Things were back to normal in her small town, as normal as they could be when you're a witch, and you've just saved everyone from a dangerous shape shifter.*

It was a good day, and all she wanted to do was go home and sleep like the dead.

The end.

I saved the document and closed the screen on my laptop. "Finished."

Stella clapped. "Yay! I'm so happy. I wasn't sure you'd ever finish that thing."

"Hey! Way to be supportive."

"I'm just kidding."

"I know."

"So, did she save the world?"

"Basically."

"You know, your next story should be some witchy fictionalized story featuring Merlock and Peter, but with a happier ending. Like maybe Esmerelda saves them before they shoot each other."

I gave her a half smile. "I might do that."

"I liked Peter, he was a good guy. Merlock, he had issues, but I think deep down, he wasn't that bad. I'm kind of going to miss them around here. Wouldn't it be nice if magic was real? Maybe things would be different if it was."

Oh, Stella, you have idea.

Witch This Way:
Holiday Hills Witch Cozy Mystery #2

Welcome to Holiday Hills, where there is magic & mystery in the air...

I wear many hats:
I'm a friend.
A sort-of girlfriend.
A ghostwriter, and…
...oh yeah, a witch.

My editor always tells me to "write what you know." Unfortunately, that's what's happening...literally.

When the main character in my latest novel—a witch herself—takes a new job with the Magical Bureau of Investigators, she stumbles upon a threat so big, it could destroy everything she holds dear.

Fiction, right? Nope.

For reasons beyond my witchy sixth sense, everything I write is now happening to me in real life!
Did I mention my character gets into REALLY bad situations?
Now I've got to figure out who's cast this awkward spell and find a way to reverse it.

And if I don't do it soon, I might just wind up the "dead" in my deadline.

Get your copy today at
CarolynRidderAspenson.com

KEEP IN TOUCH WITH CAROLYN

Never miss a new release! Sign up to receive exclusive updates from Carolyn.

Join today at CarolynRidderAspenson.com

As a thank you for signing up, you'll receive a free novella!

The Holiday Hills Witch Cozy Mystery Series

There's a New Witch in Town

Witch This Way

Who's That Witch?

The Magical Real Estate Mystery Series

Spooks for Sale

Selling Spells Trouble

Cloaked Commission

The Angela Panther Mystery Series

Unfinished Business

Unbreakable Bonds

Uncharted Territory

Unexpected Outcomes

Unbinding Love

The Christmas Elf

The Ghosts

Undetermined Events

The Event

The Favor

Other Books

Mourning Crisis (The Funeral Fakers Series)

Join Carolyn's Newsletter List at

CarolynRidderAspenson.com

You'll receive a free novella as a thank you!

ACKNOWLEDGMENTS

Thank you to my wonderful editor, Jen, my favorite proofreader, JC Wing, my amazing ARC supervisor Lynn Shaw, my fabulous ARC team, and my friends and family who've supported me as I've traveled along this writing journey. Most of all, thank you to my 'Hottie Hubby' for being my best friend and my biggest fan.

ABOUT CAROLYN

Carolyn Ridder Aspenson writes sassy, southern cozy mysteries featuring imperfect women with a flair for telling it like it is. Her stories focus on relationships, whether they're between friends, family members, couples, townspeople, or strangers, because ultimately, it's relationships that make a story.

Now an empty-nester, Carolyn lives in the Atlanta suburbs with her husband, two Pit Bull-Boxer mix dogs and two cantankerous cats, but you'll often find her at a local coffee shop people-watching (and listening.) Or as she likes to call it: plotting her next novel.

Join Carolyn's mailing list at
CarolynRidderAspenson.com

Made in the USA
Coppell, TX
04 August 2020

32384890R00099